Meg's jaw dropped. 'Are you saying you have people posted about the place to ward off anyone turning up here to take a photo of *me*?'

'We both know it's not you I am trying to protect.'

Zach's gaze was steady. Not a hint of humour. Not a hint of a smile. While Meg's cheeks grew so flushed even her teeth began to feel hot.

Ruby.

Of course. This—*all* this: the thoughtful blanket, the helpful hat, the beautiful scenery, the long brooding looks—was all about his daughter.

He wasn't thinking of her at all.

Dear Reader

This here is my twentieth book. *Twenty*. Phew! I'm shaking my head in disbelief even as I write those words.

I can still remember the moment I wrote the very first words of my *first* book, THE WEDDING WISH, and the magical moment I realised what the final line would be. My memories of feeling tumbly in the stomach and as if I was about to pass out as I sent my book to Mills & Boon in London are, as I'm sure you can imagine, less fond.

I remember so clearly the night I answered my phone and heard a gorgeous English accent. Crazy as it seemed, I just *knew* it was Mills & Boon calling. I remember the *loooong* chat with my editor before she put me out of my misery and let me know that she wanted to buy my book. Champagne flowed at my place; therefore fewer memories remain of the rest of that night ;).

I remember learning of my first title. Being told of my first release date. And, boy, do I remember finding my first box of books with my name on them at the front door. I was so excited I tore the thing open with my bare hands!

Now I'm up to number twenty. And you know what? As I sit here letting the news sink in it's truly just as exciting as the first. On that note I hand Meg and Zach over to you, and wish you as much fun getting to know them as I had.

Happy reading!

Ally
www.allyblake.com

MILLIONAIRE DAD'S SOS

BY
ALLY BLAKE

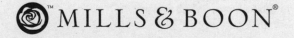

All the characters in this book have no existence outside the imagination of the author, and have no relation whatsoever to anyone bearing the same name or names. They are not even distantly inspired by any individual known or unknown to the author, and all the incidents are pure invention.

First published in Great Britain 2010
Harlequin Mills & Boon Limited,
Eton House, 18-24 Paradise Road, Richmond, Surrey TW9 1SR

© Ally Blake 2010

ISBN: 978 0 263 87662 8

Harlequin Mills & Boon policy is to use papers that are natural, renewable and recyclable products and made from wood grown in sustainable forests. The logging and manufacturing process conform to the legal environmental regulations of the country of origin.

Printed and bound in Spain
by Litografia Rosés, S.A., Barcelona

Having once been a professional cheerleader, **Ally Blake**'s motto is 'Smile and the world smiles with you'. One way to make Ally smile is by sending her on holidays, especially to locations which inspire her writing. New York and Italy are by far her favourite destinations. Other things that make her smile are the gracious city of Melbourne, the gritty Collingwood football team, and her gorgeous husband Mark.

Reading romance novels was a smile-worthy pursuit from long back, so, with such valuable preparation already behind her, she wrote and sold her first book. Her career as a writer also gives her a perfectly reasonable excuse to indulge in her stationery addiction. That alone is enough to keep her grinning every day!

Ally would love you to visit her at her website www.allyblake.com

Ally also writes for Mills & Boon® Modern Heat™!

This one's for Veronica, my constant companion
through the writing of this book—
from bump, to blinking into the light,
to becoming my beautiful smiley girl.

PROLOGUE

WWW.CHIC-ONLINE.COM.AU

News just in…

The cameras were out, the paparazzi waiting, seamstresses across the city ready to copy whichever designer frock they were about to be dazzled by, yet all were sorely disappointed when so-fabulous-it-hurts, thinking man's It-Girl Meg Kelly—the youngest, and we think most adorable, offspring of one-time uber-financier, some-time squillionaire, KInG of the corporate jungle Quinn Kelly—failed to show at the opening of hot new nightclub Bliss.

But wait, there's more!

Sources close to the family say she hasn't slept at her apartment or her folks' pad, the stunning Kelly Manor, the past two nights. And her familiar classic red convertible, often seen parked out front of Kelly Tower—the home of titanic family biz the Kelly Investment Group—is nowhere to be seen.

Where has Brisbane's favourite daughter disappeared to?

Could she be—gasp!—in hiding, nursing a new nose job? Has the nicest girl in town finally shown a kink in her squeaky clean armour by—eek!—blowing off her host? Is her vanishing act a sign that her Herculean father is not as recovered from recent heart problems as the family would have us believe?

Or—bless her little heart—has she run off with the studly Texan oil baron seen visiting the family manor last week? Oh, please, let that be it! Can we possibly hope this means the last of the Kelly kids has finally found true love at last?

Take our online poll for a chance to win a copy of bestseller Long Live the King: An unauthorised biography of Quinn Kelly!

CHAPTER ONE

'OF ALL the resorts in all the world, why did she have to walk into mine?'

Zach Jones stood in the shadows of a lush potted palm in a dark corner of the Waratah House lobby, narrowed eyes locked on the figure skipping down the wide stone steps leading away from the main building of the Juniper Falls Rainforest Retreat.

There weren't many reasons why his resort staff would contact him directly, *ever*, his reputation being that he was akin to a bear with a sore tooth at the best of times. That was as kind a character reference he could have hoped for, considering his years of un-equivocal lack of co-operation with the press.

Despite all that, the rumoured arrival of the woman currently whipping off her cap and trying and failing to tuck her mass of dark curls beneath it had been deemed important enough to give the bear a nudge.

The bear was thankful they had.

After his daily run, he'd lain in wait for her to show her face. In the end he'd missed out on that privilege. She'd scooted through the lobby, head tipped down. Nevertheless, he'd recognised her in an instant. There wouldn't be many a red-blooded man in this corner of the world who would not.

Even though she was dressed down in shorts, vest top, sneakers and cap rather than her usual society princess razzmatazz of designer frocks and diamonds, there was no mistaking her. Not with those sexy dark curls, that hourglass silhouette in miniature, the kind Zach couldn't help imagining just begged for fifties-style dresses and high heels to make the most of it, and the ridiculously confident, rock-and-roll sway of those infamous hips.

The woman who'd sent his staff into a tizz the moment she'd zoomed up to the front gates of the resort earlier that week in a growling red convertible filled with designer luggage and equally designer friends was none other than Meg Kelly.

'Dammit,' he said loud enough a group of guests heading out the doors gave him a sideways glance. He slid deeper into the shadows, a place he'd always found far more comfortable than being under any kind of spotlight.

Much less the kind of spotlight Meg Kelly seemed to carry on her person, such was her magnetism for the kind of rabid media attention usually reserved for royalty and rock stars. That kind of attention made her exactly the kind of guest most resort owners would give their right arm for.

Not him. Not now.

She disappeared for a moment behind a fat spray of red Waratah flowers and he felt himself leaning to catch her coming out the other side. He rocked himself back upright and planted his feet into the marble floor.

She popped out eventually only to bend from the waist to tug at the heel of what appeared to be brand-new sneakers, her shorts curving tight over her backside, her thigh muscles tightening, her calf muscles lengthening.

He glanced away, but not soon enough to stop the quickening in his blood. He ran a hand over his mouth, his palm rasping from the effects of three days' worth of stubble growth, and told himself it was the after-effects of his run.

He glanced back out of the window only to have his gaze catch on the sliver of pale, soft skin that peeked between the back of her shorts and her top... Was that a tattoo?

His eyes flicked to the heavens and he drew in a deep breath through his nose, attempting to temper the swift kick of attraction.

Not her. And most certainly not now.

The little-known truth that he'd stayed put in the one place for the past few months, rather than jet-setting about the globe in a constant effort to exponentially expand his empire of international resorts, would be enticing news for the kind of gossip-hungry media for whom Meg Kelly was the poster girl.

As far as he was concerned they could all go jump. Not since he'd jumped off the merry-go-round of foster homes and orphanages he'd grown up in had he let anybody tell him who he was, who he was not, how low he might fall, or how high he dared reach. His successes and mistakes were only his own to judge.

And of all the successes and mistakes he'd ever accomplished in his life the reason *why* he was now stuck in the middle of nowhere was the most inviolable yet.

In fact, he'd missed a call from his 'reason why' already that morning, and now she wasn't answering the mobile he'd bought her specifically so they could *always* be in touch.

Then his man on the ground in St Barts had left a message saying the government was playing hard ball on signing off on the final inspections of his latest resort site. And then there was Meg. All that before the day had even officially begun.

He didn't see how this week could get any worse.

Meg couldn't imagine how her week could get any better.

'Ouch, ouch, ouch!' she barked as a blister spontaneously popped up on her right heel.

Okay, so a handy supply of Band-Aids might have made it ever so slightly better, but everything else was heavenly. She simply shifted her stance to compensate and breathed deep of the glorious fresh air, sunshine and fifty acres of beautiful resort and her world was close to perfection again.

The breath turned to a yawn, which turned into a grin, which she bit back lest she be caught laughing to herself in the middle of the patch of lawn in which she'd come to a halt. Apparently she'd already been declared AWOL by the gossip hounds today—she didn't need to add loony to the list.

A funny sensation skittered down her back. Years of experience gave her the feeling she was being watched. She did a casual three-sixty-degree turn, but in the early morning, the resort grounds were quiet and still and she was all alone. It was probably just the rising sun sending prickles over her pale skin, and teasing her curls into damp springs on the back of her neck.

Another deep breath, another blissful smile as she skipped onto the immaculate lawn, which she figured would be kinder on her feet.

If her big brothers could see her now—up and at 'em before the birds, in a jogging outfit of all things—they'd be in hysterics. She wasn't exactly built for the great outdoors and her way of life meant that the only time she ever saw a sunrise was when she'd yet to go to bed the night before!

But this week she wasn't Meg Kelly, socialite. This vacation was not about to turn into some last-minute Kelly Investment Group junket in disguise. This week, thanks to her angelic best friends, she was just a girl on a summer holiday.

Sure, when Rylie and Tabitha had turned up on her doorstep two days before, told her they'd cleared her schedule, shoved her into her car and demanded she drive them to a wellness resort high in the hills of the Gold Coast Hinterland, she'd had a moment or two of panic.

Events had been planned. People had been counting on her—dress designers she was meant to be wearing, charities whose events she was attending, local businesses she was turning out to endorse, the several staff she kept in gainful employ, the women and children at the Valley Women's Shelter. There was such inertia to her life it was almost impossible to bring it to any kind of halt.

But even after Tabitha had explained that the 'wellness' in wellness resort was more about detoxing one's life by way of eating granola and valiantly trying to put one's left ankle behind one's head while meditating thrice daily, and not so much code for cocktails, chocolate fountains and daily massages at the hands of handsome Swedes she'd soon begun to warm to the idea.

As the city lights had dropped away from her

rear-view mirror and the scent of sea air had filled her nostrils the idea of getting away, of having one blissful, dreamy, stress-free, family-free, paparazzi-free, drama-free week had almost made her giddy.

Not that drama, paparazzi and family issues bothered her. They'd been par for the Kelly course from the day dot.

Though, when she thought about it, the past few months had been particularly dramatic even for her family—engagements, elopements, near-death experiences. The kinds of things that made the paparazzi that touch more overzealous, and a touch harder to avoid when she tried to sneak away for much-needed private time.

Meg shook off the real-life stuff creeping up on her and glanced back at the main building. Still no sign of the girls. Her girls. Her support crew. The ones who'd obviously sensed she was floundering just a very little even if she hadn't uttered a word. Girls who were right now both probably still fast slept in their snug, warm beds.

'Cads.'

She headed off; this time with slower, shorter steps in the hopes the girls would catch up. Soon. Please!

A resort staff member passed, smiling. 'Good morning.'

'Isn't it just?' she returned.

His smile faltered and he all but tripped over

himself as his neck craned to watch her while he walked away.

Meg's smile turned wry. So the cap and sunglasses and still-so-white-they-practically-glowed sneakers she'd bought from the resort's well-stocked shop the night before might not fool everybody as she'd half hoped they just might.

It had been a long shot anyway.

Meg stood happily at the back of the morning jogging group—primarily a group of middle-aged strangers in an impressive array of jogging outfits—collected on the track that ran along the edge of the overhang of thick, lush, dank, dark rainforest.

In an apparent effort at warming up, Tabitha lifted her knees enthusiastically high while jogging on the spot. Rylie, the Pilates queen, stretched so far sideways she was practically at a right angle. Meg, on the other hand, tried not to look as dinky as she felt without her ubiquitous high heels.

'Now that man is worth the price of admission all on his own,' Tabitha said between her teeth.

'Shh,' Meg said, only listening with half an ear as she tried to make out what the preppy, bouncy 'wellness facilitator' at the front of the large group was saying. 'Please tell me she didn't just say we're jogging four kilometres this morning!'

'She said five.'

Meg slid her sunglasses atop her cap and gaped at Tabitha. 'Five?'

'Five. Now pay attention. Hot guy at six o'clock. He's been staring at you for the past five minutes.'

'Not news, hon,' Rylie said, touching the ground with her palms and casually glancing between her legs before letting out a long, slow 'I take that back. This one is big news.'

Meg rolled her eyes. 'I'm not falling for that again.'

'Your loss,' Rylie said.

A husky note in her best friend's voice caught Meg's attention. 'Fine. Where?'

'Over your right shoulder,' Tabitha said. 'Faded T-shirt, knee-length cargo shorts, sneakers that have pounded some miles, cap he ought to have thrown away a lo-o-ong time ago…'

Rylie laughed, then gave Meg's leg a tug so her knee collapsed, turning her whether she wanted to or not.

Meg didn't even get the chance to ask Rylie what was so funny. She didn't need to. There was no way any woman under the age of a hundred and twenty was going to miss the man leaning against the trunk of one of the massive ghost gums lining the resort's elegant driveway.

He was tall. Impressively so. Broad as any man she'd ever met. His chin was unshaven, the dark curls beneath his cap overlong. With the colour of a man who'd spent half a lifetime in the sun and the muscles of a man who hadn't done so standing still, he looked as if he'd stepped out of a Nautica ad.

She tucked a curl behind her ear and casually bent down to tug at her ankle socks, not needing to look at the guy to remember exactly what she'd seen. Her hands shook ever so slightly.

He was the very dictionary definition of rugged sex appeal. For a girl from the right side of the tracks, a girl who was a magnet for stiff, sharp, striving suits, a girl whose planner had become so full of late she had to diarise time to wash her hair much less anything more intimately enjoyable, he was a revelation.

She glanced up as she stood. He hadn't moved an inch.

The skin beneath her skimpy clothes suddenly felt hot, and the fact that it was thirty-odd degrees and muggy had nothing to do with it. She was a Kelly, for Pete's sake. It took something *extra* extraordinary to make a Kelly sweat.

Though she couldn't see his eyes beneath the brim of his soft, worn cap, she could feel them on her. Her right shoulder tingled. The sensation moved up her neck. It finally settled in her lips. The urge to run her fingers across them was so strong she had to curl them into her palms.

Then he finally moved. He pressed away from the tree and shifted his cap into a more comfortable position on his head before crossing his arms across his chest. His strong, tanned, brawny arms. His broad chest.

She breathed in deep, releasing it on a long, slow, deliciously revitalising sigh.

What if *this* was what she needed more than even a holiday right now? More than granola or t'ai chi. More than early-morning jogs or internal reflection classes. A little bit of something for herself.

Could she? Should she? Considering every step and every misstep she experienced outside the walls of her family home somehow ended up being known by the whole country, it took something *extra* extraordinary for her to put herself out there. The lanky stranger who would not take his eyes off her was exactly that.

She took another deep breath, faced him square on and gave him an honest, inviting, unambiguous smile.

Needless to say, after all that build-up, it was more than a bit of a shock when she didn't get one in return. *Nada.* Not a twitch, a nod, not any kind of acknowledgement that he was paying her any attention at all.

Her cheeks heated from the inside out, her fingernails bit into her palms, and her lungs suddenly felt very, very small.

Meg fair leapt out of her skin when Tabitha leant on her shoulder and sighed. 'Imagine,' she said, 'if we hadn't kidnapped you to this place this moment never would have happened.'

'I'm trying my very best to imagine it right now,' Meg said on a mortified croak.

Pathetically late though the attempt at saving face was, Meg let her gaze glance off Mr Tall Dark and Silent Rugged Man, then up into the sky as if she were pondering the time and using the sun as her guide.

'I might well be seeing things,' Rylie said, finally upright and now staring brazenly at the silent stranger, 'but isn't that Zach Jones?'

Meg grabbed Rylie by the hand and spun her around to face front. All the while her wits began to return and synapses connected in the back of her brain. 'Why do I know that name?'

Rylie said, 'He was a rower years back. Olympic level. Keeping it up too, by the looks of him. Now he's a businessman. Big time. Owns this place, in fact, as well as a dozen-odd of its like all 'round the world. Self-starter. Self-made. Renegade. Refuses to list his company on the exchange. Not all that much known about him otherwise. He somehow manages to live under the radar.'

'Single?' Tabitha asked.

'Perpetually,' Rylie said with a grin.

'Perfect.' Tabitha grinned. 'Your dad'll hate him.'

Meg turned on her. 'So?'

Rylie said, 'She has a point. You don't have to limit your dating schedule to charming, skint, ambitionless, undemanding men to get back at Daddy.'

Meg's right eyebrow tweaked to a point. 'I actually *prefer* to spend time with men who don't consider bragging about that day's corporate buyout fit for pillow talk, thank you very much. I get enough of that around the family dinner table to find it in any way an aphrodisiac. The only way my father comes into it is that at least men not on their way up the corporate ladder never try to get to him through me.'

Tabitha mirrored her expression. 'Whatever you say.'

Meg poked a face, then looked decidedly back to the front of the group.

What she didn't say was that the men she favoured also weren't the types to press for any kind of commitment. They weren't in any rush to start families of their own. One less pressure to concern herself with.

Besides, it had been a long time since she'd bothered doing anything extreme in order to get through to the big man herself. What was the point? It had never worked anyway.

Rylie pushed in tighter, her voice a secretive stage whisper. 'It has to be him. Zach Jones. He's notoriously impossible to pin down. He's one of those ungettable interviews that would take a girl like me out of Sunday morning fluff TV into the big leagues. I wonder what he's doing here rather than flitting around the world buying up great wads of prime real estate like it's going out of fashion? I smell a scoop.'

Meg shook her escaping curls from her cheeks and peeked out of the corner of her eye one more time.

He'd tilted his head up ever so slightly. Sun-kissed skin was smoothed over the most immaculately masculine bone structure Meg had ever seen. The shadow of three-day growth covered a jaw that just begged to be stroked. And his lips were so perfectly carved she struggled to take her eyes off them.

All that perfection somehow managed to pale in comparison when she finally saw his eyes.

They were locked on hers.

Dark, dangerous eyes, too far away for her to make out the colour, but she had the feeling she could have doubled the distance between them and still been hit by the thwack of awareness behind them.

She sucked in a breath, thick with tropical humidity that caught in her throat. And a trickle of what was most definitely sweat ran down her neck and between her breasts.

Zach Jones.

His name buzzed about inside her head in her father's most frosty voice as he flapped the *Financial Times* in a way that meant he was not happy. '*He got too big, too quick. Stubborn fool is overreaching. One of these days he'll land flat on his face. Mark my words.'*

Meg didn't know about overreaching, but she did know that her father didn't give a damn about *anyone* below a certain level of accomplishment—client, competitor, offspring...

She swallowed.

There was no flirtation in Zach Jones's gaze. No measure of awe about who she was. Just copious amounts of brooding intensity centred in those unfathomable dark eyes. Despite it all, the backs of her knees began to quiver.

He blinked. And rolled his shoulders. The first sign he wasn't as nervelessly blasé as he was making out.

The very thought made way for an unimpeded rush of sexual attraction to slide through her, like a waterfall breaking through a dam of knotted foliage that had held it back a decade.

The ferocity of her reaction had her literally taking a step back. The blister on her heel popped, again. A hiss of pain slid through her teeth as she hopped madly on her good foot.

The man took a step towards her, a hand appearing to flicker in her direction. The tension curling inside her ratcheted up a notch and a half and she knew her sudden breathlessness had far less to do with her stinging foot, and more to do with the stranger in her midst.

Thankfully she caught her balance all on her own, and the man unclenched from his ready-to-pounce position.

She spun back to face front. 'When are we going to start running, for Pete's sake?' she whispered through her teeth.

Rylie reached out and pinched her hot pink cheek. 'Look who's suddenly Miss Eager Exerciser.'

'You bet,' she said, shuffling from one foot to the other as though she had ants in her pants. 'Bring on the lactic-acid burn!' Better that than having to endure the feel of the man's burning eyes on her back.

She shook out her hands, attempting to shake off the fidgets. It wasn't as though she hadn't been rebuffed before. It came with the celebrity package as much as being excessively adored. It just thankfully generally happened from afar. By strangers. Whom she didn't have to look in the eye and pretend it didn't sting.

'Meg, he's coming over!' Tabitha said so loud those straggling nearby must have heard.

'We'll leave you to it, then,' Rylie said cheerily. 'I'm counting on you to get me the exclusive!'

'No, no, no!' Meg begged.

But it was too late, they were off—Rylie the runner, and Tabitha the gym junkie. There was no way Meg was keeping up with them, even with the amount of adrenalin pouring through her body as she stood all alone in the middle of the dirt track, Zach Jones making a beeline her way.

CHAPTER TWO

MEG jogged for almost five minutes before pulling up to a walk. By then she was already wishing she'd brought a better bra, a hairband and a scooter.

The rest of the stragglers passed her by, including the wellness facilitator who had been bringing up the rear.

All bar one.

She could feel a male presence tucked in behind her. She could hear the heavy pad of his large feet on the compacted dirt path. Dragging in deep, unfit breaths, she caught his scent on the hot summer breeze—expensive, subtle, and wholly masculine.

All this from a man who'd managed to get under her skin in half a second flat. A man who'd rejected her come-hither smile in even less time. Sheesh. The sooner she found out what he was after and got rid of him, the better.

She said, 'Are we there yet?' just loud enough he could have no doubt she was talking to him.

'Do a U-turn and ask me again,' a deep voice rumbled beside her. A voice that matched the rest of him so perfectly that if she wasn't gleaming with perspiration from the effect of it she deserved some kind of medal in self-control.

Meg pinched her side with the hopes of fending off an oncoming stitch and the slow burn of attraction that was infusing her in one fell swoop, and turned.

At a distance Zach Jones was something. Up close and personal he was too beautiful for words. Her breath shot from her in a discombobulated *whoomph*.

She concentrated on the slight bump of a once-broken nose, the different angles each of his dark brows took above his hooded eyes, the stray sun-kissed flecks within his dark hair, lest she be overwhelmed by the whole.

'Please don't hang back on my account,' she said, oft-practised casual smile firmly entrenched. 'My pace is purposeful. Those chumps up ahead don't realise how much more one can appreciate the scenery by walking.'

He said, 'I'm fine right here.'

If she didn't know better she could have taken those words a whole other way. As it was she had to give her heart a mental slap for the unwarranted little dance it was currently enjoying.

'Excellent,' she said. 'We'll walk together. Scenery is always more enjoyable when you have someone to share it with.'

And then neither of them said another word for a whole minute. The unmistakable tension was almost enough for Meg to start jogging again, despite the fact that she'd barely caught her breath.

'Would I be right in thinking you're not a big runner?' he finally said.

After Meg's laughter died down she waved her hands in the direction of her well-tended curves. 'Do I look like a runner?'

Given the invitation to do so, the man's eyes travelled down one side of her body—over her borrowed hot-pink short shorts and black T-shirt with sparkly designer name splashed across her chest—and up the other. Given the chance, she looked into his distracted eyes.

Deep, dark, soulful brown they were, with the kinds of creases at the edge that she just knew would make a girl's heart melt at ten paces when he smiled. *If* he smiled, which she realised he still was yet to do. In fact, he carried with him the distinct impression of a frown.

Finally, and none too soon, Meg managed to duck out of the heady cloud of attraction to hear cymbals crashing inside her head. They warned of impending doom.

There was no doubt he was intentionally at her side. He'd had to have waved the wellness facilitator on to get her alone. But it was becoming increasingly clear he wasn't exactly over the moon to be there. On both counts she was clueless as to why.

She worried the tiny chip in her front right tooth with her tongue, an old habit that re-emerged only when she felt as if things were slipping out of her exacting control. An old habit she worked hard at keeping at bay.

She curled her tongue back where it belonged and answered her question herself. 'Between us, running's not my forte. I'm more of a yoga girl.'

Sometimes. Every now and then. Okay, so she'd taken a couple of lessons with Rylie once.

'Yoga,' he repeated, his eyes finally, thankfully, leaving the contours of her body and returning to hers.

She shouldn't have been so thankful so soon. For in those dark, deep, delicious brown eyes she saw that he had seen the equivocation in hers.

She dropped her gaze to the fraying collar of his T-shirt lest he see the surprise in her eyes as well. She'd had a lifetime in which to perfect the art of being Meg Kelly, public figure. Her front had been demonstrably shatter-proof. *Two minutes* after meeting her, Zach Jones had seen right through it.

Who was this guy and what did he want with her?

'Downward dog? Upward…tree?' she shot back, arms swinging in what she knew was a terrible impression of something she'd seen on TV once. 'Okay, so I'm not a yoga fanatic or a runner. I'm more an eat-chocolate-for-breakfast dance-it-off-in-your-living-room kind of girl. Either way there is no way on God's green earth I'll be catching up to the others any time soon. So please go ahead. Jog. Be free.'

'Between us,' he said, leaning in, his voice dropping to a conspiratorial tone that sent her blood pressure soaring, 'I've already run five K today.'

'Oh.' Oh, indeed. 'So what brings you out here again?'

All she got for her blunt question was an out-held hand. 'I'm Zach Jones.'

Meg twisted her body to slide her smaller hand into his. Even the coolest of customers usually gave themselves away when shaking her hand. A nervous vibration here, a sweaty palm there. She was extremely adept at ignoring their nerves.

With Zach Jones they never eventuated. His grip was warm, dry, strong, masculine and wholly unmoved.

Remarkable, she thought. More than remarkable. The man was perspiration-inducing, utterly gorgeous and wholly unsmiling even though he had the kind of warm, open, likable face purpose built for the function.

And don't forget, she reminded herself, *beneath the casual curls, the sexily shabby clothes, and the body of an Olympic god, Zach Jones is an alpha in beta camouflage. So not worth worrying about.*

So why was she still holding his hand?

Because it really is so very warm, dry and blissfully enveloping, that's why.

'I'm Meg,' she said, pumping once more, then letting go.

At the last second she held back her surname. As if there was a slim chance she'd been reading too much into every cheek flicker, or lack thereof, from the very beginning. Maybe he was just some cute guy too shy to chat her up even though he had a thing for girls with impossibly curly hair and a glaringly obvious lack of sporting prowess.

'It's a pleasure to meet you, Meg,' he said, his mouth quirking at her omission.

Argh! What was she thinking? He knew. Of *course* he knew. She'd have to go further than the Gold Coast to find a man who didn't know who she was. A man whose mind wasn't already made up about her before they even met.

She squeezed her eyes shut a moment. Using a technique they'd encouraged in internal reflection class the day before, she searched for her centre. Patience thin, she failed miserably. Instead she went with what worked in the real world: she summoned her inner Kelly and looked the guy dead in the eye.

'So, Zach Jones, from what I hear around the traps you own this joint.'

The full-frontal approach brought out a combative glint in his darker than dark eyes. If possible it only made the guy more tempting. Warmth curled through her empty stomach.

But rather than doing the polite thing and answering her charge, he ignored it and asked, 'How long are you planning on staying?'

Frustration began to war convincingly well with attraction. In response, her practised smile only grew wider.

'A survey?' she said, lobbing it right back in his corner. 'Aren't you the hands-on boss?'

The most sensuous mouth she'd ever laid eyes on kicked into a sexy almost-smile, creating an arc in his cheek that hinted at so much more, but still it never quite reached his eyes. He didn't believe her devil-may-care performance for a second.

'How long?' he repeated.

'We're here the week.'

His eyes skimmed the empty path ahead. 'We being?'

Something in his tone gave her the sense the impending doom wouldn't be impending that much longer.

She casually lifted a foot and stretched her... whatever the muscle that ran down the front of your thigh was called. 'Two of my closest mates gave me this holiday as a present. Rylie Madigan and Tabitha Cooper.'

At the last second she threw out their full names

on a gamble, for Tabitha, with her ex-Prime Minister dad, and Rylie, with her job on TV, were almost as recognisable as she was.

Her fishing paid off. He breathed deep, his fists bunched at his sides, and the sexy hollows in his cheeks grew their own hollows.

'So you go home…?' he said.

'In a few days.'

He nodded, breathed out deeply, apparently most satisfied that she'd be out of his sight as soon as that.

Whoa. That was harsh.

Even though beneath the bright smiles and fancy clothes she was a tough cookie—she had to be in order to survive being a Kelly—it turned out she was still just a girl whose pride could be hurt like anyone else.

Okay, so there had been a time before she'd toughened up. A time when she'd been in danger of imploding under the relentless pressure. A long time ago, a lifetime really, in some perverse effort to get her father's attention she'd let things go far too far. It had scared her enough to buck up and take control over her image, her life. To figure out how to use the process that used her.

Any naivety she might have had was lost for ever, making a certain amount of cynicism unavoidable. On the upside she was no longer easily fazed. By anything.

Yet somehow this guy was getting to her.

Frustration finally won out, bringing with it a desire to share the pain. She lifted her chin and breathed deep of the tropical air. 'I have to say you picked a gorgeous spot here. I could really get used to it. Who knows? We may stay longer yet.'

His eyes slid back to hers; dark, gleaming, shrewd.

She raised both eyebrows. *Now what are you going to do about that?*

What he did was smile.

Naturally it was everything she'd imagined it might be and so much more. The latent vitality his physique hinted at shone from his eyes when he smiled. It made him appear playful, warm, engaging. Her knees turned to jelly. Her resolve turned to mush.

She opened her mouth, ready to ask him outright what the hell was going on when he placed his bare hand in the small of her back and gave her a light shove. She was so surprised she gave a little yelp.

Through the thin cotton of her T-shirt his fingers were hot. Insistent. Touching her without fear or favour.

Only when she looked up to see a small tree in the middle of the path did she realise he was merely stopping her from thwacking into the thing.

And even after his hand moved all too easily away, and even while he was making her feel more and more out of step with every step in his presence, she could still feel the hot, hard press of Zach Jones's hand against her skin.

Now why did he have to go and touch her?

A simple, 'Watch out for the tree,' would have sufficed. Instead, constant glimpses of that tattoo peeking out from the rise of her shorts had been like a magnet.

Now he had to do this thing with the sensation of that soft warm skin imprinted on the tips of his fingers.

Zach curled said fingers into his palm and took a small step to the left to add a little more physical distance between himself and the woman at his side. The woman whose very proximity could expose everything he'd worked so hard to keep pre-served. Protected. Pure.

He stretched out his shoulders and shot her a sideways glance. He had to concede that for a woman who appeared to bloom under the spotlight like an orchid in a hothouse, in person she was smaller, more low-key, and more approachable than he'd expected her to be. Funny, mischievous, switched on…

He actually had to remind himself her father was Quinn Kelly, one of the most patronising men he'd ever had the displeasure of dealing with in the early stages of his business career. No doubt there would be a good dash of spice beneath the sweet. That kind of bite had to be genetic.

As for the rest of her?

His gaze lingered on her mouth before skimming over her pale bare shoulder, down her slim arm, over her Betty Boop hip, before being drawn back to that mouth.

Surely lips that lush could not be the real deal. Soft, pink, curving up at the corners even when she frowned as she was doing right then. Those lips alone were enough to make sure half the men of Brisbane thought themselves in lust with her. The other half simply didn't read the right papers. And as it turned out *his* body didn't give a hoot if they were genuine. Saliva gathered beneath his tongue. He swallowed it with such force his throat ached in protest.

His gaze moved north only to be reminded of those infamous blue eyes. The colour was mentioned every time her name was spoken aloud. The second she'd turned them his way he'd known why. They were startling—glinting, bright, sapphire blue. The kind of blue that looked as if it could cut glass. The kind of blue that could make even the most disinterested man dive right in and not care if he drowned.

Luckily for him the fact that his hormones had so spectacularly tuned into Meg Kelly's siren song was not going to be a problem to add to the reasons why he needed her as far away from there as possible. He'd long since been wise to the barb of wanting someone that would never be his to have.

He had the relentless dislocation of his childhood to thank for that vital life lesson if for nothing else.

There was no getting away from the fact that she was trouble. Add friends who were of all people a TV reporter and an ex-Prime Minister's wild child to the mix and his day had just got a whole lot worse.

It was time to turn things around.

'Ms Kelly,' he said, making sure she knew without a doubt he knew who she was, 'I need you to tell me what you and your friends are really doing here.'

Her hands clenched so tight at her sides her knuckles turned white. Whatever else she was, Meg Kelly was smart. She had clued onto the fact that he wasn't about to roll out the red carpet.

'Whatever do you mean?' she asked, her spicy core all too evident in her tone.

'Wouldn't you all prefer somewhere more… rousing in which to spend your vacation?'

She afforded him a glance. There was nothing he could pinpoint to say it wasn't a perfectly amiable glance. Yet he felt the smack of it like an arrow between the eyes.

'I'd say a five-thirty wake-up call is about as *rousing* as I like things to get when on holidays,' she said.

His cheek twitched. He corralled it back into line. 'Perhaps. Yet neither you nor your friends fit into our usual demographic of guests looking to shed a few pounds, get back to nature or affect a mid-life change of life.'

He turned to find she had come to a halt. Hands on hips. She said, 'Now why would you think that we aren't here to replenish our emotional wells just as it suggests on the brochure? Is my jogging prowess really that atrocious?'

Her answer was entirely reasonable, her tone playful even. But in the end it was those most famous of eyes that gave her away. Inside she was readying for battle. A battle he had no intention of letting her win.

He took a slow step inside her personal space, forcing her to tilt her head to look up at him. He could feel the breath from those sweet lips brushing over his chin. His blood accelerated with the kind of urgency it hadn't felt in a good many months.

'A private island off the Bahamas,' he said. 'A yacht on the Mediterranean. Las Vegas. You could be in any of those places within twenty-four hours and no jogging would be required.'

'Well, now, *Mr Jones*,' she said, her voice low and deliciously smooth. 'I'd think twice before making that your new resort motto.'

Again his cheek twitched, and again he caught it just in time. He leaned in as close as he might without risk of contact. Her chin shot up, her jaw clenched, her stunning blue eyes flashed fiercely.

His skin warmed, not like a man with a serious

purpose, but like a man in heat. He pulled hard at a hunk of leg hairs through his shorts.

'Then what do you think of this one? My resorts are places of private contemplation and rejuvenation, not celebrity hunting grounds. If I see one film camera, one news van, anything that looks like a long lens glinting through the underbrush—'

'Then what?' she said, sitting on enough steam to cut him off. 'You'll assume it's somehow our fault and kick us out?'

God, how he would have loved to have done just that. But negative publicity would bring as much attention to the place, and to him, if not more.

'Of course not,' he said, turning down the heat. 'I'm only concerned that your privacy remains upheld as much as I am concerned for the privacy of all of us staying on the resort grounds.'

She watched him for a few moments, her eyes flickering between his as if she was trying desperately to figure out his angle. She could try all she liked. She would never know. Her jaw clenched tighter again when she realised as much.

Then with what appeared to be an enormous amount of effort she breathed in, breathed out and smiled so sweetly his whole body clenched in anticipation.

'So no drunken nudie runs across the golf course. No demanding that everything we eat is first washed in Evian. No insisting a documentary crew follow our every move for a new reality TV show. Then we can stay?'

He lifted his eyebrows infinitesimally in the affirmative. 'That works for me.'

She lifted hers right on back. 'Truly, Mr Jones, the further away you stay from the marketing side of your businesses, the better.'

Then *she* took a step closer, this time purposely invading *his* personal space. He dug his toes into his shoes to stop himself from pulling away from the rush of her body heat colliding with his.

'This is your lucky day,' she said. 'Because I am here for a holiday, not to be caught out in my bikini for next month's *Chic* magazine gossip pages. This is my first real vacation in a little over two years, and I need it. I really do. So for the next few days I have every intention of having a fun time with my friends. Right here.'

She pointed at the dirt and looked up at him, daring him not to believe her. But even though she appeared to be the very picture of candour, he had too much at stake to care.

'And your friends—?'

'Exist entirely independently of me.'

It was not an ideal answer, but he'd done all he could do without holding her down and forcing her to give him her oath in blood. He said, 'Then I bid you have a wonderful stay for the remainder of the week.'

She nodded. And when she finally took a slow step back he felt as though a set of claws was unwinding from his shirtfront. The waft of hot summer air that slid into the new space between them felt cool. Cooler at least than the remnant reminder of her body heat.

She started to walk away, talking back to him as though expecting him to follow. 'You know, there is something you could do to make sure my stay is wonderful.'

Negotiation? This he could do with far more panache than stand-over tactics. In three long strides he was back at her side. 'What's that?'

'The mini-fridge in my room is stocked with nothing but bottled water. I'd re-e-eally like you to add some chocolate to the menu. And coffee. I'm not fussy. Instant's fine. Not you personally, of course. You still have to catch up to the group ahead to survey them as to why they're here and to wish them all a nice stay too. They are already about a kilometre ahead of you so you'll have to run your little heart out to catch them up.'

And then Zach laughed, the sound echoing down the unoccupied tunnel ahead. Well, that was the very last thing he'd expected he might do after he'd first answered his phone that morning.

While her forehead frowned, her mouth curved into a smile. A smile with no artifice or strategy. A smile that reminded him of one she had aimed at him while he'd been standing in the shade of the gum trees awaiting his moment to strike. A smile that even from that distance he'd recognised as being loaded with pure, feminine summons.

He swallowed the last of his laughter and cleared his throat before saying, 'If you *had* read the brochure you might have discovered that this here's a health resort.'

'So that's a no?' she asked.

'Unfortunately, that's an absolute no.'

'Oh, well. I guess it never hurts to just ask nicely. Right?'

The hint in her tone—that he might have caught more flies with honey—was as subtle as a sledge-hammer, but by the time he realised it she'd lifted her feet and jogged off along the trail, her dark curls swinging, the small muscles of her thighs and calves contracting with each charmingly wonky step. If she made it back to the main house before lunch he'd be very much surprised.

Zach slid his mobile phone from his pocket, called the resort's manager and asked him to contact the wellness facilitators to send someone to escort her back to the resort.

He flicked to his inbox. No new messages. No more missed calls. His frown lines deepened so severely he wasn't sure they'd ever fully recover.

Then he turned tail and ran in the opposite direction.

He concentrated hard on the *whump whump*

whump of his feet slapping against the compacted dirt. Better that than let himself get caught up in that earlier moment of unmistakable invitation. Or the lingering spark.

He pushed himself harder. Faster. Till sweat dripped into his eyes. It didn't help.

Maybe if she'd lived down to his expectations and been the ditzy powder puff he'd fully assumed she'd be, that'd be the end of that. Instead he couldn't let go of the fact that despite her reputation she'd been out there at six in the morning with no entourage, no make-up, no airs and graces, no expectation of special treatment.

A woman who hid a sharp tongue behind her soft lips. A woman whose wickedly intelligent eyes could make lesser men forget themselves.

Zach pushed till his muscles burned.

Forgetting himself was not an option. It would mean forgetting a little girl who had no one else left in the world to protect her bar him.

His daughter. A daughter only a handful of trusted people even knew about.

No one else *could* know. Not yet. Not now.

She was so very young. Her life so recently upheaved. It was all he could do to keep her safe.

To do that he had to keep her from those in the media who would carelessly make bold, loud assumptions about her future before she ever had the chance to find her footing in the present.

He knew full well how even the most innocent of

comments at that age could influence how one thought about oneself. He'd met more than one person in a position of power who'd taken some kind of sick pleasure in telling a lonely orphan kid that he was nobody and would grow up to be even less. Decades on he still remembered each and every one.

He'd never forgive himself if that happened to her because of her relationship to him. And that meant keeping her identity concealed from those for whom Meg Kelly was their most prolific source of sustenance.

Eyes on the horizon, he ran until his shins ached, his heels felt like rock, and his body was drenched in thirty-five-degree sweat.

He ran until the ugly faces from his past became a blur.

He ran until it no longer mattered how long he'd now been in lock-down in this middle-of-nowhere place trying to make his round life fit into a square hole.

He ran until he was too exhausted to be concerned that he was trying to be a father when, having never had one himself, he had no real clue what the word meant.

He ran until he could no longer quite remember the exact mix of colours it took to make up the most bewitching pair of feminine blue eyes he'd ever be likely to see.

CHAPTER THREE

POST-BREAKFAST, post long hot shower, make-up done, hair coiffed, and changed into a vintage pink designer sundress—the exact kind of body armour she'd have preferred to have been wearing when meeting the likes of Zach Jones—Meg's skin still felt all zingy.

Not good zingy either. Uncomfortable zingy. Miffed zingy. It didn't take any kind of genius to know it was all *his* fault.

Standing in front of Waratah House she held the resort map in front of her, turning it left ninety degrees, then right. Rylie and Tabitha thought she was taking a nap, as they were. All the zinging made that absolutely impossible, so she'd snuck out.

'Excuse me?' she said to a passing couple. 'Do you happen to know which way's north?'

The gent pointed without even thinking. Amazing. Then his hand remained outstretched, his mouth agape even after she'd hit the bottom of the wide steps and was heading north towards the bulk of the resort, her ballet flats slapping against the stone path.

Her calves were so tight she winced with every step. The blisters on her heels stinging as if they were teaching her a lesson for not wearing high heels.

Message well and truly heard, she wasn't going to push her luck by going the week without her beloved caffeine as well. She was going to find something sweet and dark and rich and bad for her if she had to hike down the mountain, flag a passing truck and barter her shoes for some at a local milk bar.

The fact that what she craved sounded a heck of a lot like Zach Jones only made her walk faster.

It really was the strangest thing. She was used to people bending over backwards to get her endorsement, to have her wear their product, mention their charity, look sideways at whatever they were touting. Not that she ever agreed unless it was something she'd advocate even without being asked.

Zach Jones, on the other hand, had all but suggested he'd really prefer it if she and her friends would just clear off. To Las Vegas, no less. As far, far away from his resort as possible seemed to be his main point.

Far, far away from him.

Yet there was no mistaking the zing of electricity when he'd touched her. No denying the way the tension vibrating throughout him had melted away when she'd made him laugh. No confusing the way he'd taken his time getting to know her body when she'd unthinkingly told him to take his fill.

And absolutely no doubting, whatever beef he had with her, it was very *very* personal.

She was nice, for Pete's sake! She worked her backside off. She was kind to small animals. She gave everyone a fair go. Why shouldn't she expect to be treated the same way?

It was as though the guy had been given a torch and a map pointing him right towards her Achilles heel—a terminal relic of a childhood spent doing whatever it took to get even a hint that her father cared. *That* heel couldn't be soothed with antiseptic cream and Band-Aids.

'Grrrrr!' she shouted to the wide-open sky.

When she glanced down a group of guests in matching pale green Juniper Falls Rainforest Retreat brand tracksuits doing t'ai chi on a mound of grass were looking her way. From nowhere one of them pulled out a mobile phone and took her picture.

It shouldn't have surprised her. It happened every day.

But being on holiday she'd been silly enough to let down her guard. Enter one tall, dark, handsome businessman and her usual cool had gone up in smoke. She had to pull herself together quick smart.

The kind of attention that followed a down-and-out It Girl was far worse than for one who went about her business with cheerful grace. Not only would that adversely effect the family—God, the horror of ever being on the end of *that* conversation—the one part of her life that was truly her own, her one beautiful unspoiled secret, her time volunteering at the Valley Women's Shelter, would be gone.

Zach Jones was a very lucky man. They both seemed to want the same thing—for this next week to be drama free. She'd just have to keep Rylie away from Zach, Zach away from Tabitha, and herself aware of the whereabouts of all three so that she could relax. Ha!

Meg picked what felt, and tasted, like birdseed from between her teeth. If she was looking for a reason to really not like him she realised she had one. It was his fault her belly was full of nothing bar raw oats bathed in pale soy milk, bite-sized chunks of some mysterious organic fruit and a green drink so thick and speckled it looked as if it had been scooped out of primordial ooze.

She needed chocolate. And coffee. And bad.

She pulled herself together and waved cheerfully to the group. 'Good morning, all!' she called out.

A few people waved back. Several more mobile phones went click-click before the wellness facilitator clicked his fingers loudly and reminded them it would be best to leave their mobiles in their rooms while working towards a mind free of distractions.

Then she skipped up the path as fast as her sore muscles and flat shoes would carry her.

Skirting the eastern edge of the resort grounds, Meg passed an array of cosy guest bungalows peeking out of the edge of the rainforest. One was completely covered in creepers, the next had been built on stilts above a bounty of ferns. Another bungalow had obviously been built around an existing tree. Each was more charming than the last. But unless the gingerbread house from Hansel and Gretel appeared next she wasn't slowing.

Coffee, chocolate, coffee, chocolate, chugged in her mind along with each step. The large outbuildings she'd seen on the map had to contain food for the staff. Food she planned on sweet-talking her way.

A handful of minutes later Meg's foot slipped a tad and she realised she was no longer on the white stone path that guided guests everywhere around the resort. Thicker, less perfectly trimmed grass slid underfoot. And the rainforest encroached more tightly on all sides.

She was so hot she was puffing like a steam train. Her brow, her underarms, and the spots behind her knees were slick with sweat. And she realised she had no idea where she was.

A gap appeared in a moss-covered rock wall peeking through the underbrush ahead. A faint path had been beaten into the grass at her feet by regular footsteps so she did all she could think to do and followed.

Barely a dozen steps beyond she found herself in a garden—tiered, and lush with wildflowers in the most amazing, vibrant colours the likes of which she'd never seen.

And beyond that…

A house. But what a simplistic word for the structure crouching silently before her.

A large octagonal structure had been built tight against a rising embankment. It had a pointed thatched roof and more windows than walls. Rope bridges led from the yard up to the front door, and then again from the front door to several separate enclosed rooms scattered haphazardly about the hill face. A meandering creek ran beneath, and a wide deck wound around the lot.

Her brother Cameron, the engineer, would go absolutely nuts for the place. She just stood there and admired the heck out of it, not noticing a rhythmic squeaking sound until it stopped.

She glanced towards the space where the noise had been to find a young girl staring at her. Her small hands were wrapped about the handles of a swing, legs locked straight as she used her feet as a brake to halt her progress through the air. Her long dark hair was pulled back by a yellow headband and flickering in the light breeze.

She must have been six or seven, around the same age as her brother, Brendan's eldest girl, but with her loose footless pink tights and pink floral shoes browned by mud she was deliciously messy where Violet and Olivia were always picture perfect. As always happened when unexpected thoughts of her favourite girls came to her, Meg's heart gave an anguished little skip. The skip was always part love, part fear.

Right now they were such innocents. But without their mum around any more to give them balance they were becoming deeply indoctrinated into the Kelly way of life. Meg's greatest hope was that somehow, some way, they would have a choice in how their lives turned out that she'd never had. And that being the granddaughters of Quinn Kelly didn't eventually smother those sweet natures for good.

'Hi,' the young girl said, and Meg blinked to find herself on the other end of a long, flat, intense stare.

Shoving her concern for the next generation deep down inside where it couldn't shake her, she took a deep breath and smiled.

'Hiya,' Meg said.

The little girl shuffled her feet through the muddy ground till her legs dangled beneath the rubber swing and her hands slid down the chains. 'I'm Ruby,' she said.

'It's a great pleasure to meet you, Ruby. I'm Meg.'

Ruby's mouth twisted as she fearlessly stared Meg down. Meg bit back a smile. She was being sized up.

When Ruby came back with 'I'm seven and a half,' she knew she'd come up to muster.

'Seven and a *half*? That's impressive. I'm a tad older than seven too, and I'm lost. Any chance you can read a map?' Meg waved hers back and forth.

Ruby merely blinked at Meg, giving her time to work out the answer for herself.

'No?' Meg slowly tucked the map back into the front of her dress. 'Fair enough. I couldn't read a map at seven any better than I can now.'

From nowhere her father's voice came to her. *How simple do you have to be not to be able to tell up from down, girl?* She placed a hand over her thudding heart and begged it to calm down.

And for good measure found herself, once again, cursing Zach Jones.

It was *his* fault the resort menu contained nothing remotely normal, thus sending her out into the blinding heat in search of sustenance. It was his indifference that had made her crave comfort chocolate in the first place. He'd started the chain reaction that was bringing up long-since-buried feelings now fanning out like a swarm of angry bees whose nest had been poked with a really big stick. She had no idea what one was meant to do to mollify angry bees, but as for her…

Her hand fell limply to her side as she sniffed the air. 'What's that heavenly smell?'

'Chocolate muffins,' Ruby said. 'My nanny cooks them. I don't like muffins much.'

'You don't like muffins? And you call yourself a seven-year-old!'

Ruby's mouth quirked ever so slightly. Her eyes narrowed for several moments before claiming, 'My dad likes them so I get her to make them for him so he can take them to work and I just eat the leftovers.'

'I see.' Meg licked her lips and looked to where the smell was coming from. The sight of that dramatic dwelling reposing peacefully, silently, privately within the forest had her letting out a long, slow, soothing breath. 'That is one amazing house you have there, Miss Ruby.'

'It's not mine. It's my dad's.'

Meg's eyes swerved back to Ruby to find her toes had slunk together, her chin had dropped and her whole body had curled into itself.

With Violet and Olivia firmly in mind, Meg made sure she had the girl's full attention before she said, 'You have your own bedroom, right? Fridge privileges. Access to the TV remote.'

Ruby thought a moment, then nodded.

'Then that means it's your house too.'

Ruby looked up at the house thoughtfully. Meg did the same, wondering how close the kitchen might be. And if she might be able to outrun the nanny. Then it occurred to her—it was mid-morning on a weekday.

She spun back to Ruby. 'Shouldn't you be at school?'

Ruby's mouth puckered into a defiant little pout and her chin lifted a good two inches. 'I have a sore throat.'

Meg's eyes widened as she let her gaze run over the swings, and the Frisbee resting next to them on the lawn. If the kid had a sore throat she'd give up chocolate for ever. Still, Ruby's rebellious streak hooked her. Maybe the kid was more like her than her nieces after all.

'A sore throat, you say.'

Ruby nodded, then added a couple of terrible attempts at a sniffle for good measure.

'You know what?' Meg said, tapping her chin with her finger. 'When I was seven and a half and got a sore throat, I found the days went so much quicker if I actually went to school. I know, sounds crazy, huh? But truly, by the time I got home I'd forgotten all about my throat and why it felt sore in the first place!'

Ruby eyed her down a moment before admitting, 'It has been a very long day.'

Meg laughed before hiding it behind a cough. 'Okay, now the lesson's done, you didn't hear this from me. But if I did stay home from school I let my mum smother me with ice cream and tuck me up with blankets on the couch while I watched daytime TV. That way she knew where I was and I felt better at the same time.'

Ruby blinked, but her expression didn't change a jot as she said, 'My mum's gone.'

'Gone?'

Ruby nodded.

And then Meg knew from the look in the kid's eyes 'gone' meant she wasn't coming back. She took a step towards the small girl and knelt down in front of her. 'Oh, sweetheart.'

Why God let some kids grow up so quick she'd never understand. Now she *did* understand.

Now she did understand the sore throat all too well. Classic 'get Daddy's attention' manoeuvre. But come on, what kind of father didn't give his little girl attention when he was the only thing she had left?

The guy obviously had no idea Ruby's attention-seeking behaviour could escalate so fast and in ways more dangerous than he would ever believe possible. Then again, maybe he knew, and maybe he simply didn't care.

Meg nibbled at her bottom lip as she glanced back to the house. This wasn't some shell shocked urchin at the Valley Women's Shelter happy to have a pair of warm, comforting arms around her no matter who they belonged to; this was a spunky, healthy-looking kid, surrounded by toys in a multimillion-dollar home. A home Meg was currently trespassing on.

She stood and took three steps back. 'Sweetheart, I'm sure your dad knows where the ice cream is kept too.'

This time at mention of her father Ruby sat bolt upright. 'He's busy. He has an important job with lots of people counting on him. He works all week while I'm at boarding school and only comes home weekends when I come home. But I could go get him now if I really wanted to. To tell him about my throat and all. I just don't want to.'

'He works at the resort?' Meg asked. The imaginary huffy bees were back, swirling about her head with increased volume and intensity.

Ruby said, 'He owns this one and lots more all over the world. He's going to take me on his plane and show me all the others one day. He promised. Just not right now. I have school when I'm not sick. But some day.'

Meg heard not much more than *blah blah blah* as she stared down at Ruby. The dark hair, the wary dark eyes, the natural intensity that even a supposed sore throat couldn't dampen. Once she saw the similarity it was so blaringly obvious she felt like a fool for not noticing it sooner.

Her blood pounded so loudly in her ears her voice came out rather more flat than she would have liked when she said, 'You're Zach Jones's daughter.'

Ruby's eyes flashed with the first spark of real

enthusiasm and Meg knew she was right ev
before the girl said, 'Do you know my dad?'

Did she know Ruby's dad? Not a jot.

*Zach Jones had a daughter. A daughter whose
mother was gone.*

Hang on, he had a daughter with a mother Rylie
hadn't even known about and Rylie was such a pro-
ficient muckraker she probably already knew who
really killed JFK and was awaiting the right
moment to reveal all.

He had a daughter who was at home sick, or pretending to be. And the only reason Meg saw that
Ruby might not want him to know was in case he
only proved to her he didn't give enough of a damn
about her to care.

Meg's fists clenched at her sides, a scene to end
all scenes threatening to erupt from within.

She'd seen it time and again listening to stories
told by countless women at the Valley Women's
Shelter—men, focused on themselves, on their
work, on their local bar, who blithely disregarded
their children's need to be loved. Hell, she'd seen
it with her own eyes. She'd felt it with her own
heart.

Thankfully she'd taken measures in order for it
never to happen to a child of her own. Conclusive
measures. Unfortunately none of that helped her
from feeling threadbare watching neglect happen to
someone else.

Her gaze cleared to find Ruby was still looking up at her with her father's uncompromising gaze. And while she knew the second she'd found out who Ruby's dad was she should have walked away, she still said, 'As a matter of fact I met your dad only this morning.'

'What did he say about me?'

What did he say? Well, he was actually pretty darned arrogant. He said back off. He said lie low. He said…

Meg's fingers unfurled from her palms. He'd said he was determined that the privacy of *all* staying at the resort remained upheld.

He was talking about himself. Him and his anonymous daughter. A daughter who no longer had a mum.

She closed her eyes to hide the mortification that she had beamed her flirty little smile at a man who'd lost his…wife? Lover? Ex? What did it matter? He'd lost the mother of his child.

Far too many adult-only concepts to share with a seven-and-a-half-year-old.

Instead, she gathered up her cheeriest smile and said, 'I'm such a yabberer I'm sure I didn't let him get a word in edgewise. If he'd had the chance I'm sure he would have said plenty. How could he not? A daughter who lets her nanny make chocolate muffins even though she doesn't like them but her dad does. You're a gem!'

Ruby tried for a smile herself, but her sr.
shoulders drooped, giving her away. Meg's hea.
twitched far harder than she liked for the little girl.
She couldn't let herself get attached. There was no
way it could end well.

She opened her mouth to say her long-overdue
goodbye when something out of the corner of
Ruby's eye had her springing from the rubber seat
like a jack-in-the-box. 'I have to go!' she shrieked.

Meg glanced up at one of the small detached
rooms to see the wooden blinds snap shut. A flash
of silver hair, not dark and curling, meant her heart
didn't stop, but it certainly thundered hard enough
for her to know she'd pushed her luck far enough.

Ruby took a last quick step forward. 'You won't
tell my dad I was on the swings, will you?'

Meg laughed. 'Not a chance.' Probably best for
her continued health if she didn't bring any of this
up with the man at all.

'I won't tell him you were here either, okay?'
Ruby said.

Meg laughed again. 'That would be fine with me.'

Ruby gave a quick, sweet, girlish wave, and then
ran off towards the flickering blinds and freshly baked
chocolate muffins, her long hair swinging behind her
as she skipped up onto the longest rope bridge and
was soon consumed by her astonishing home.

Meg spun on her heel and vamoosed back along
the makeshift path, through the gap in the rock wall

out onto the manicured grass of the resort
oper. She headed in a direction she thought was
probably south. If it wasn't, someone would put her
to rights soon enough.

Her breaths shook as the adrenalin she'd held at
bay finally spilled over.

What if when she'd smiled her flirty little smile
Zach had smiled back? What if when she'd made
him laugh she'd let herself join in? What if when
he'd touched her he'd liked it too much to let her
go? What if things had happened between them
and she'd gone in deep before he'd decided to let
her know that he had a little girl?

It had taken her nearly thirty years to get to the
point where she finally felt as if she had a handle
on her celebrity. There was no way she would
knowingly expose a child to it.

It gave her the perfect excuse to wash her hands
of the whole situation, get on with her holiday, and
forget the lot of them even existed.

Damn him! He'd started this. By including her
in his convoluted duplicity he'd made her a part of
it. And having met Ruby, talked to her, looked in
her eyes and seen herself mirrored right on back she
couldn't let it go.

He might not know it yet, but Zach Jones needed
her help. And for the sake of a bright, sweet,
adoring little girl who needed him it appeared he
was going to get it.

CHAPTER FOUR

MEG rushed to find the Wellness Building to meet the girls for that day's internal reflection class. While they tried to locate their *chi* she had every intention of pretending to meditate while dreaming up the perfect way to broach the subject of his daughter when she bumped into Zach Jones again.

With an objective in sight, despite the flat shoes and sore muscles, she had a decided spring in her step when she rounded a thick bank of head-high reeds.

Until she came face to face with a human rear-end.

Male it was, bent from the waist. Knee-length khaki cargo shorts sculpted a magnificent rear belonging to a tanned, solid man fiddling with something in a cooler. And even though she couldn't see the colour of his hair, or the breadth of his shoulders, or the shape of his arms or any of the other bits that seemed to be permanently imprinted on her mind, she knew it was Zach Jones.

Her heart hammered in her ears, and her palms grew slick. She and *chi* might well be incompatible, but there was simply no denying this man's life force was so potent it radiated from his very pores.

He stood, stretching out his limbs. Sunlight glistened lovingly off the expanse of perfectly sculpted muscle, as he was naked from the hips up.

His large hand was wrapped about a condensation-covered bottle of beer. He tilted his head and downed half the bottle in one slow go.

Meg's gaze remained stuck on the muscles of his throat, pulsing with each large swallow, with each heavy thud of her heart against her ribs.

Once done, he let out a deep, satisfied *ah-h-h* that seemed to echo across the distance between them, then he wiped a tanned, muscular arm across his forehead. He might as well have been sliding that arm around her waist for the reaction that shuddered through her.

'I must have done something horrible in a previous life to deserve this,' she murmured beneath her breath.

As though the slow, hot, summer air carried her whisper to him too, he stilled. Then his body twisted at the waist until his eyes locked on hers.

The colour of expensive dark chocolate. The colour of strong espresso coffee. Right there in those eyes she saw everything she hungered for. Unfortunately half a second later she also caught the full force of his disapproval simmering beneath the urbane surface.

Then she remembered why.

She'd been seriously kidding herself in thinking she might be able to convince this man he needed her help. If he had any idea she'd stumbled upon his daughter he'd probably already decided which exact spot in the surrounding rainforest would be the best place to hide her cold dead body.

Her tongue darted nervously out to slide along the chip in her tooth. His gaze slipped to watch the movement, his dark eyes turning almost black.

She was pinned to the spot, unable to move as he reached out and grabbed a T-shirt from beside the cooler, then slid it on in that particular way men did such things. The soft cotton casually sculpted his muscles and if at all possible he was even more intimidating fully dressed.

When Meg finally found her voice again she said, 'This isn't the way to the Wellness Building.'

'No,' Zach said, his deep voice rumbling through her very bones. 'It's not.'

She frowned. 'Where am I exactly?'

'The lake.'

'There's a lake?' she asked. 'Wow, I really don't know how to read a map.'

'I'll give you a hint,' he said. 'It's the big blue bit at the bottom with "Lake" written in the middle of it.'

Her cheeks, if possible, grew warmer still. Her voice was dripping with sarcasm when she said, 'Thanks. You are as ever the gracious host.'

'Was there something else you wanted from me?'

'Look, you can relax. I really didn't mean to invade your beer-drinking time. Stumbling upon you was pure accident.'

'Obviously fifty acres isn't quite as much room as it sounds.'

'So it seems.' She began to back away. 'If you'd be so kind as to point the way—'

'I was just about to head out for a row. Want to join me?'

Her feet stumbled to a halt. 'Excuse me?'

While his eyes seemed to skim the view behind her in search of prying eyes, he waved an inviting arm towards the end of a jetty that was shrouded in tall reeds wilting in the heavy heat. 'After many months of wrangling with a guy on the end of the phone, my old row boat has finally arrived from a storage lock-up in Sydney and I'm taking her for a spin. You game?'

Game for *what*? Concrete shoes? A speedboat containing Rylie, Tabitha and their ready packed bags? Or worse, an intimate boat ride with a man whom she couldn't want; who didn't much like her; who still managed to give her uncontrollable stomach flutters that only grew more intense with each and every meeting.

A whimper from her self-preservation instincts had her licking her lips in preparation to say thanks but no thanks, until her mind filled with the memory of a sprawling house in the forest, and a lonesome, brown-haired girl with his eyes.

The most decisive reason for her to walk away was the one reason she finally could not.

'Sounds lovely,' she said with the distant but polite smile she used on those who shamelessly accosted her in the fruit and veg section of her local supermarket asking for an autograph.

His eyes darkened all the more, as though he knew it too, but he still slipped the strap of the cooler over his shoulder, then turned and walked towards the lake.

Meg did all she could do and followed.

Once she rounded the thick reeds she saw a small, fat, wooden boat bobbing merrily on what turned out to be a massive lake. The boat's mission-brown paint was faded, the red floor was scratched and fatigued, and the benches had seats worn into them from a lifetime of accommodating bottoms.

It was ancient and imperfect. So not the kind of sea-faring-type vessel any of the men in her family would be caught dead in. She loved it.

She crouched down and ran a hand over the stern to find it smooth and soft. 'She's really yours?'

She glanced up to find Zach watching the rhythmic movement of her hand. She curled her fingers into her palms and pushed herself back to standing.

He had to bend past her to unhook the rope from the jetty. She leant back to give him room, but not far enough not to catch his scent. She breathed it in. She couldn't help herself. It was drinkable.

He wound the rope around his hand and elbow, muscles contracting with every easy swing. '*Marilyn*'s been a faithful companion since I was about eighteen.'

'*Marilyn*? Are you serious?'

His cheek twitched into one of those almost smiles that gave a girl unfair hope there might be more to come. 'She came with the name.'

'Sure she did. You haven't thought to trade her in for a fancy schmancy yacht with all the trimmings?'

'I've got one of those too. A hundred footer moored off St Barts right now.'

'The *Norma Jean?*'

And there it was. The holy grail. His mouth tilted into a slow smile complete with brackets that arced around his beautiful mouth and creases fanning out from the edges of his delicious dark eyes. Boy, were they worth the wait.

'I called her *Lauren.*'

'Bacall?'

'It was my mother's name.'

Of course it was. Meg looked down at her shoes

instead of into those too discerning eyes. 'And a tad extravagant to use for a paddle about the lake.'

'Just a tad.'

She glanced up, and for a brief moment Meg swore she saw a glint warm his dark eyes before it was gone. He ought not to bandy those about unless he meant them. It was hard for a girl not to get ideas.

Zach threw the rope into the boat, then held out a hand. Unless she wanted him to know her mouth turned dry at the thought of him touching her again, she had no choice but to take it.

A slide of natural warmth so out of sync with the constant cool in his eyes leapt from his hand to hers. She gripped on tight as she stepped into the wobbly vessel, but the second she had her backside planted on a bench she let go.

He stepped in after her and tossed her a cosy, red-checked, woollen blanket. It was too soft to be freshly washed, too fluffy to be new. It was the kind of thing a man might keep at the end of his bed, or the back of his couch. She imagined it covering his long bare legs as he lay back—

She cleared her throat. 'What exactly am I meant to do with this?'

'Slide it beneath your backside or you'll get splinters,' he ordered. 'That or that dress of yours will be shredded.'

Of course. So what if it carried a faint lingering

scent of him—he hadn't given it to her as some sort of come-on. It was near forty degrees out! She lifted her backside and planted it back on the folded blanket.

'This too,' he demanded, throwing her a soft khaki fisherman's hat, which was frayed to the point of falling apart.

She gripped the hat between tightly coiled fists. All that commanding was beginning to get on her nerves. Her voice was sugary sweet as she asked, 'And where, pray tell, am I supposed to put this?'

His hands stilled. He glanced up. The smile hovered; the glint loomed.

And it hit her as if the lake had suddenly thrown up a tidal wave over the boat. Zach Jones might prefer her to be far, far away, but a certain part of him took a purely masculine pleasure in having her close by.

She licked her suddenly dry lips and blinked up at him. The smile faded and the glint disappeared without a trace.

'Just stick the thing on your head, will you?' he growled.

'Aye aye, Captain,' she muttered.

The hat smelled like the sea and fitted over her head like velvet. Atop her sateen cocktail dress it must have looked a treat.

He slapped an old cap atop his curls, shoved a foot against the jetty, pushing them off before easing down onto his own bench.

She tucked her knees tight together and pretended to pay attention to the ripples fanning out through the flat silver water, and not how close his knees were to hers, as he picked up the oars and pushed them effortlessly out into the lake.

Within seconds the wilting reeds shielded them from the rest of the world and they were alone.

The sun beat down upon Meg's back, making her glad of the hat. The soft swish of the displaced water created a slow, even rhythm. And as Zach built up a sweat every breath in gave her a fresh taste of his clean cotton clothes and some indefinable heat that was purely him.

Like this, all easy silence, all effortless masculinity, it was hard not to imagine he might be exactly the kind of guy she could happily spend oodles of time with. A beautiful sailor who slept in late, didn't believe in making plans, and just went with the flow.

It was hard to believe he owned and ran a huge multinational business that no doubt took long hours away from home. That took the kind of relentless ambition that meant everything else in life came a distant second. Family included.

Her brother Brendan was trying to do the single father thing. Running the Kelly Investment Group and raising two young daughters. And though she'd never tell him so to his face she knew in her heart the half of his life he was letting slip from his grasp was his girls.

Zach's eyes slid from some point over her shoulder to find hers. His dark, deep, unfathomable eyes. Their gazes held a beat longer than polite. Two beats. She held on, trying to sense regret, bereavement, concern for his little girl. All she got for her trouble was the sense that *she* was getting more entangled by the second.

She breathed in slow and deep through her nose. Could she ask him about Ruby now? Should she? Would she be doing it to be helpful? Or did she know he'd react badly, so she could use Ruby to save herself from feeling the way she did when he looked at her like that?

In the end she lost her nerve and said, 'So you've been on two runs today and now rowing. I feel tired just thinking about it.'

He went back to staring at the water. 'I like to be on the move. Eyes forward, nothing but the wind and the sun to keep me company. It clears the head. If you don't run or do yoga, what do you do?'

Mmm. She had proven that day that exercise made her hurt, and wobble and crave sugar.

'To clear my head?' she said. 'Disco music.'

One dark eyebrow rose and his hot, dark gaze slid back to hers. 'Disco?'

'Blaring from my iPod directly into my ears. Ten seconds into any Donna Summer or Leo Sayer song and the rest of the world fades away.'

They said music soothed the savage breast, and so

it had done for her, many a time in her teens when she might have otherwise given in to mounting frustration with her life and done something she'd later regret. Ultimately disco could only soothe so much hurt.

'Even if you're lying on the couch your feet can't help but bop. Your head clears of everything but the music. It's kind of like exercise only more relaxed.'

When he merely blinked at her she gave him her 'greeting line' smile, with a full showing of teeth, twinkling eyes and dimples. 'You're going to give it a go the moment you go home, I can tell.'

And while most people, even members of her own family, could no longer tell when she was 'on' and when she was just being herself, the slow rise of the corner of his mouth told her she hadn't fooled him for a nanosecond.

How did he *do* that? How was *he* able to see straight through her? Again she felt exposed, as if she'd walked into a ballroom with her dress tucked into the back of her undies.

He stopped rowing and the boat's sleek glide slowed so that she rocked forward on her seat.

'I'm game. I'll give disco a go,' he said 'But only if you take the oars right now.'

She imagined splinters. She imagined aches in even more as yet undiscovered muscles. She imagined her hands brushing against his as she took him up on his offer.

'I'll pass.'

Zach laughed. The column of his throat moved sexily beneath the sound. It faded all too soon in the wide-open space, and his eyes once again grew so dark they drew her in while they pushed her away.

She wondered if he could see the same impulse in hers.

She wondered what might happen if they both pulled at the exact same time.

His large hands curled back around the worn old wooden sticks and he slid the oars back into the water, pushing off with such grace and power Meg was sent to the back of her seat. Smart move. Pushing was much more sensible.

A cooling wind fluttered past her warm face. Streaks of gold dappled the rippling silver water where the sun burst through fluffy white clouds. The edges of the lake were completely obscured by the thick, green rainforest spilling into water.

Time stretched and contracted. She realised she had no idea how long she'd been gone. Or why he'd taken her out there onto the lake alone in the first place.

'I don't mean to say this isn't entirely pleasant, and so generous for the owner to give me such a personal tour of the blue bit on the bottom of the map,' she said, 'but how long were you planning for this outing to be?'

'We can turn back now if you're getting too hot.'

Only then did she even consider that, while he

looked like a sun god, she must have looked an utter treat—in his floppy hat, her hair plastered to her face after her hike to the end of the resort and back, her Irish skin pink as a rose.

She wasn't used to feeling so discomposed; her voice was rather sharper than she intended when she said, 'I'm only thinking of you.'

He raised a solitary eyebrow. 'You're thinking of *me*?'

More than you know. 'Many a poor fellow has ended up reportedly engaged to me after spending far less time in my company, and I have been made quite aware how highly you regard your privacy.'

'I do at that. Which is why I have not left any stones unturned in an effort to protect it. You needn't worry on my behalf.'

'I need not?'

His cheek twitched. 'The forest has eyes. Trackers flushing out the perimeter in search of poachers.'

'Poachers? There's nothing for miles bar a few birds, some lizards and a bunch of resort guests in matching tracksuits.'

And then she got it. Her jaw dropped. 'Are you saying you have people posted about the place to ward off anyone turning up here to take a photo of *me*?'

'We both know it's not you I am trying to protect.'

His gaze was steady. Not a hint of humour. Not a hint of a smile. While Meg's cheeks grew so flushed even her teeth began to feel hot.

Ruby.

Of course. This, *all* this, the thoughtful blanket, the helpful hat, the beautiful scenery, the long brooding looks, were all about his daughter.

He wasn't thinking of her at all.

Zach couldn't remember a time in recent history when he'd been so furious. And mostly with himself. For since the moment he'd turned and found Meg Kelly standing on the jetty in her completely inappropriate pink party dress he'd thought of nothing but her.

He hadn't been exaggerating when saying he rowed to clear his head. The sport had saved him from being just another scrappy, angry kid with a chip on his shoulder and had turned him into a man who knew how to focus, create goals and push himself to the absolute limits to achieve them.

He needed a clear head now more than ever. The St Barts government was still playing hardball with the building inspections on his latest site. It was balanced on a knife's edge with his only achievable contributions controlled by the whims of local telephone operators. Because he was trying to run a multimillion-dollar international business from a laptop and a three-room bungalow in the middle of nowhere.

For Ruby. So she could be in a familiar place. So she knew her world was solid and secure. Ruby, who, despite his best intentions, had been compromised.

When Ruby's nanny had called to say she'd had a visitor he'd almost popped a gasket, believing the woman had blatantly gone out of her way to punish him for not bowing and scraping and rolling out the red carpet. When he'd calmed down he'd realised the only way she could possibly have found Ruby in such a short amount of time was by stumbling out of the forest in one great cosmic accident.

Either way, rather than putting himself as far from Meg Kelly as he could, he now had no choice but to be on her like a rash until the day she left.

So as far as he was concerned Meg Kelly could sit out in the hot summer sun all day, her knees knocked in chagrin, her ridiculous dress getting splattered with water spray, his dilapidated green hat sloping low over her face, leaving only her down-turned mouth in sight.

Except of course it had only given him enough time studying that mouth of hers to know it was all natural. And so was she. Her skin was as pale as it ought to have been with a smattering of freckles across her nose make-up couldn't, and needn't, hide. Her curves were as God gave her with apparently a little bit of help from occasional disco. The woman was pure, wholesome femininity and irrepressible audacity and ingenuous sex appeal.

He was beginning to wonder if she'd been sent to test him. After dedicating his entire adulthood to purely selfish pursuits, was he really man enough, strong enough, self-sacrificing enough to resist her? To put aside his needs for the needs of one girl?

When Ruby had landed on his doorstep, her small hand held tight in the hand of a weary-looking social worker, she was alone in the world, orphaned and in shock. She'd been on the verge of replaying his cold, lonely, disjointed past through her future. There was no way he could let that happen to her and look himself in the mirror ever again.

But had he been the right person to save her?

He let out a long, hard breath and realised that beneath the brim of his hat Meg was watching him. Those sharp blue eyes constantly calculating.

He should have known better than to believe what he'd heard about her in the press. Assuming she'd be a lightweight adversary had been a huge tactical error. It served him right that it had come back to bite him where he'd feel it most.

The ante had been upped. It was time he showed his cards.

He used the oar on the starboard side to head the boat back to civilisation. 'So, Ms Kelly.'

'Yes, Zach.'

'What possessed you to trespass inside my private residence this morning?'

'Your yard,' she shot back as though the words

had been waiting to explode from inside her. 'I never went any farther than the very, *very* edge of your yard. Once I knew it was yours I was out of there.'

'I don't give a flying fig if you were sitting on my rooftop. What the hell were you doing so far from the boundary of the resort that we now have to have this conversation?'

'Please,' she scoffed, her voice cool, her eyes electric. 'It was an honest mistake. It's not like there's a ten-foot-high electric fence separating the two.'

'There's a rock wall and a whopping great big gate!'

'A gate? Not today there wasn't.'

Zach swore beneath his breath. That meant Ruby had been out again. What would it take to make the kid understand that it was for her own safety that she stay put and not gallivant about the resort? Hell, all he wanted was to keep her clear of those who would have her believe that because her childhood had not been perfect she was damaged from the start. He was fast running out of ideas.

The boat rocked beneath them as he pulled harder on the oars. Meg's hands whipped out to the sides and held on tight.

'For a woman who thinks lying on the couch listening to disco is a form of exercise, the hike to my place makes no sense.'

'Fine,' she said, throwing her arms in the air, rocking the boat so that he had to steady them with some fancy flicking of the oars. 'I was casing the grounds in search of chocolate.'

'Give me a break—'

She lifted her chin as though a haughty bearing could make the words seem less undignified. 'I warned you. Caffeine is a staple in my diet. And I never expected to have to go cold turkey this week. So actually it was all your fault that I ended up there.'

His laughter again came from nowhere and again surprised the hell out of him. And a few local birds that screeched as they scattered from the treetops nearby.

Gorgeous, plainspoken and stimulating. Delilah herself couldn't possibly have been more tempting.

Thankfully he'd long since proven himself invulnerable to the lure of apparently easy promise. He'd learnt early on not to trust the feeling as far as he could throw it. So long as the bright, breezy, easy warmth in this corner of the world hadn't rotted away his indoctrinated dubiousness he'd be just fine.

CHAPTER FIVE

'ZACH,' Meg said, and by the tone in her voice Zach wasn't sure he'd be keen on what came next.

'Okay,' she continued, 'I was hoping to get around to the fact more gracefully, but since I have no idea how long you intend to keep me hostage out there let's get to the point. You have a seven-year-old daughter named Ruby who, it seems, nobody knows anything about. There. Now it's out there. So what do we do from here?'

Zach slapped an oar into the water at such a rough angle it covered them both in wet spray. 'Don't get cute, Ms Kelly.'

She waved a hand across her face as though swatting away a fly. 'Stop being so formal. I've practically been in your house, I'm on first-name basis with your daughter, and you've seen me in this hat. Call me Meg.'

Through gritted teeth he said, 'If you saw yourself in that hat you wouldn't be half so concerned.'

She blinked up at him. Hell. So much for proving himself invulnerable. Now she was sitting there gawping at him as if he'd outright told her how lovely she was.

'Okay then, *Meg*,' he said, his voice coarse, 'if formalities are now to be tossed aside, then I'll be blunt.'

'All this time you were being polite?' Something in his expression must have made her catch her tongue. She mimed zipping her mouth shut. That mouth…

'I want you to tell me in avid detail about every second you spent in my daughter's company. And don't miss a moment.'

She blinked at him. 'Relax, Zach. We didn't talk about sex, drugs or rock and roll if that's what you're worried about.'

Sex? *Drugs*? He ran a hard hand over the back of his neck, which suddenly felt as if it were on fire.

'She's seven, for Pete's sake. The *High School Musical* soundtracks are as extreme as her rock and roll tastes go.'

She hooked a thumbnail between her teeth and looked up at him from beneath her thick dark lashes. His gut sank so fast he pressed his feet into the bottom of the boat. What wasn't she telling him?

By age seven he'd already stolen his first pack of cigarettes, he'd kissed his first girl, he'd been hit so hard by one so-called parent he'd gone to school with a hand print bruised into the back of his thigh.

He'd known Ruby barely seven months. There was a fair chance he didn't know his kid at all. His voice was unsteady as he said, 'Ruby's situation is…sensitive, therefore it's imperative that I'm kept informed.'

'Just informed? Not present? Not available? Not her first port of call?'

The riddles finally became too much and his frustration got the better of him. 'Meg, I'm her father. If I don't know everything I'm going to imagine the worst and then go quietly out of my mind.'

A smile spread across her face—a radiant thing that made the sun beaming down upon the lake pale into insignificance. 'Well, now, that's just about the best news I've heard all day.'

He shook his head, hoping for clarity. None came. 'What on earth are you talking about?'

'The fact that you *want* to know is a good thing. A wonderful thing.'

She even reached out and patted his hand, as if he'd accidentally given her the password to a treasure he didn't even know existed. It wasn't the kind of touch he wanted from her.

'Then hurry up and tell me.'

'I'm not going to break her confidence that way. Come on.'

Zach glanced at the clouds above Meg's head. Who in heaven had he screwed over to be made to live through this day?

'Trust me,' she said, 'every girl needs her mysteries, especially from her father. It's character building. So long as she knows you care enough to *want* to get to the bottom of them, to the bottom of her, then you have nothing to worry about.'

Nothing to worry about.

She couldn't possibly have known that of all the four-word combinations that could placate his exasperation with her, that was it.

Still, time and again in his life, just when he'd begun to get comfortable, that was when fate pulled the rug out from under him. Foster families he'd felt as if he'd connected with had let him go. His knee had given way a week before the World Championships and he'd been forced into early retirement from competitive rowing. The momentum and success of his resorts had him finally living his life in such an easy groove, then along came Ruby.

He couldn't accept things could be that simple. That certain. There always had to be a catch. What was he missing?

Aw, hell.

'What did you tell your friends about her?'

'Nothing!'

'One thing I've learned from Ruby is that girls like to talk to their friends. A lot. About everything.'

'We do. A lot. But here's the thing—I have the feeling the reason you accosted me this morning was tied up with wanting to keep your private life separate from your working life. And Ruby would naturally be a big part of that. Right?'

He didn't say no.

'If so, believe me, I'm not going to be the one to out her. She's your only secret kid, I assume. Lone heiress to all this?'

Zach still didn't say no.

Meg said, 'Well, I know better than anyone what she'd have in store for her if the world found out. I wouldn't bring it on any young girl.'

Crazy as it sounded, he believed her. 'Thank you.'

'My absolute pleasure.' She smiled. That lush mouth. Those stunning blue eyes. He had a sudden need to know what they'd look like bathed in moonlight as she spilled apart in sheer pleasure in his arms.

He hooked the oars back into their loops and aimed for the resort, and every stroke felt as if he were pulling them through wet cement. 'You seem perfectly comfortable in the limelight. Are you implying that's all an act?'

'Oh, no, did that just sound all woe is me? Please tell me it didn't. Don't get me wrong, I know I'm blessed in, oh, so many ways. And I am perfectly at peace with the contradictions that came with being notable. But I wasn't born twenty-nine and world wise. You haven't heard the story of my glittering debut?'

Zach shook his head.

'Well, here it is. I must have been three at the most. My father was giving a press conference to announce that he'd bought the George Street building in which the Kelly Investment Group was housed and was renaming the thing Kelly Tower. Mum had taken us all along to see him in action. All trussed up for the big occasion, my hair in ringlets, wearing my favourite navy velvet dress and black patent shoes, I got away from her. I made it to the podium mid-announcement, clambered up, tugged on my father's trousers and whistled through the gap in my front teeth that I needed to tinkle. Needless to say my father wasn't all that impressed at being upstaged, but the press ate it up. I haven't been able to tinkle since without the world knowing about it.'

Her smile was cheeky, but as he seemed able to do with this woman from the outset he felt the undercurrent stronger than the surface words. On the outside it was a cute story about a girl and her dad. For her it was a story of innocence lost.

He pulled the oars harder through the water. 'Just because a spotlight follows you doesn't mean you have to perform for it.'

She raised both eyebrows in challenge. 'You really believe that? Do you really want to know the God's honest truth? Or are you pushing my buttons in an effort to continue to punish me for the whole Ruby thing?'

He felt a smile coming, but this time didn't bother trying to put a stop to it. 'Both.'

'Fine.' She took a breath. 'The only reasons I am telling you any of this is recompense for Ruby. Okay?'

'Okay.'

'Fame is a funny old thing. It's not like I've done anything to deserve being remembered. I haven't invented something, or cured anything or broken any world records. But my name has brand recognition, which gives me not only a certain power, but responsibility as well. Say the name Kelly and what do you think?'

Wealth. Charm. Beauty. But also excessive influence. Secrets. Lies. Scandal. Everything he wanted Ruby nowhere near.

She didn't wait for him to answer. 'I had to figure out early on how to deal with all that baggage. I have no interest in running the company like Brendan. Or owning the city like Cameron. And the rush Dylan feels every time a new client is lured into the KInG net is a mystery to me. I wouldn't even begin to know what drives King Quinn himself. But what I can offer with a splash of perfume, a flash of designer skirt and a dash of feminine glamour is a much-needed counterpoint to the excess of testosterone my family exudes. A way to use some of that power for the greater good. And, boy, am I good at it. So good I could sell tickets. But unless you know a guy with a good line in wigs and fake noses it's twenty-four hours, seven days a week, barely a holiday in sight.'

'Why do it at all?'

She blinked, clearly thinking him obtuse. 'For them. For each other.'

'For your family?' That kind of self-sacrifice was something he was only just beginning to understand.

'Jobs change. Friends come and go. Family is where you begin and where you end. My brothers may appear to be the kings of the jungle, but deep down they have the hearts of big kittens. They need me as much as I need them. And no matter what part we play all of us are working towards the same goal.'

'The succecss of your father's business.'

'No. For our family to be happy. The business success is a side effect. I certainly don't dance to my father's tune, if that's what you mean.'

'Is that what I said?'

She frowned deeply. 'It's what you intimated, isn't it? To be fair, I did once. Then a time came when I became a right little tearaway. The things I got up to would make your eyes water. Then I grew up. Took charge of my life. And decided making love and not war was the only way forward.'

'Who knew the life of a society princess was lived on the front line?'

Her frown faded away, but her eyes remained locked on his, a tad wider than normal, as though she couldn't quite believe she was telling him all of this. 'You can mock me all you like, but in offering a corner of myself to those who are interested, I am able to use my money, my influence and my time helping some of the less trendy, less telethon-appropriate organisations I believe need all the help they can get, which is extremely satisfying.'

'I wasn't mocking you. I—'

What? *Envy you your infamously close family?* Like hell he was going to tell her that.

Not knowing how to ask, he instead said, 'Moving on.'

'Excellent idea.' She let out a deep breath and leant forward, just a touch, but enough that when her mouth curved into an all-new smile, a luscious, flirtatious, brain-numbing smile, he felt it like nothing else. If her life really was lived on a battleground, that mouth was as good a weapon as they came.

'Am I off the hook?' she asked.

He slowed his strokes, not quite ready to return to land. To real life. To the other side of the battle from her.

'Just one last thing. Tell me how you got the chip in your tooth.'

She crossed her eyes as her tongue slid to the gap. His hands gripped the oars for dear life.

'It's so tiny. How did you even notice it?'

'I happen to be an extremely perceptive man.'

Her eyes slid to his, warm, tempting, wondering

just how perceptive he might be. Unfortunately he was perceptive enough.

As she slid her tongue back into her mouth her teeth scraped slowly over her lips and her nostrils flared as she let out a slow, shaky breath. He knew he wasn't the only one feeling the impossible zing between them. He also knew she was wishing with all her might that he hadn't noticed a thing.

She tilted her chin up a fraction before shaking her hair off her shoulders in a move meant to distract him from the fact that for the first time since he'd met her she was no longer looking him in the eye. 'How else would a party girl chip a tooth but on a glass of champagne? On the upside, it was truly excellent champagne.'

He laughed softly as he was meant to do. Her eyes flickered to his and her smile was grateful.

After a few long, loaded moments, Meg asked, 'I just…I'd like to know one thing too. Did Ruby tell you I was there?'

He shook his head. 'Her nanny.'

She nodded, then looked down at her paint-chipped fingernails with an all-new smile on her face. A secret smile. An honest smile. One reserved for Ruby.

And from nowhere Zach felt something the likes of which he'd never felt in his entire life—the most profound kind of pride that a woman such as her thought so highly of his little girl.

* * *

Meg's tongue kept straying to the itty-bitty chip in her tooth.

What had she been thinking, fessing up to all that guff in some great unstoppable stream of consciousness? Nobody wanted to see the workings behind the wizard. It ruined the fantasy. It seemed all she needed was a man who looked her in the eye and asked about the real her, and it was fantasy be damned.

Thank goodness she'd been rational enough to pull back when she had. There were some parts of her life not for public consumption.

If she wanted to continue volunteering at the 'less trendy, less telethon-appropriate' Valley Women's Shelter she had to keep it underground too. Every woman needed her mystery, and every public figure needed their sanctuary, even if it meant she had to truss herself up in a blonde wig, red liptick, brown contacts, and tight second-hand acid-wash jeans circa 1985.

If she was to remain Brisbane's favourite daughter she had to pretend the part of her life in which she'd attempted to leave the spotlight had never happened. She felt lucky much of her memory of that time was a blur of flashing lights— from the nightclub, the police car, the hospital.

As to the way she had finally taken control of her life? If she planned on going through life with a spring in her step and a smile on her face she knew it was best not to revisit the choices she'd made back then ever again.

It was done. It was for the best. Move on.

So Zach Jones—stubborn, pushy, scarily insightful Zach Jones; the guy who saw through her so easily that every time they met she had to chase him deeper into the darkest recesses of herself in order to drive him back out—could just take a step back.

Besides, her big mission had been to sort him out, not the other way around. *He* was the one with the rebellious daughter. *He* was the one who'd lost someone close. *He* was the one who needed help.

As she'd seen real social workers do, she started slowly, easing her way to the point so as not to scare him away.

'So Ruby was home sick from school,' she said. 'Does that happen a lot?'

Zach's cheek clenched and the look in his eyes made her wonder if he might not be deciding whether Operation Dispose of Meg might have to be put into action after all.

'I ran away from home once when I was a little older than her,' she pressed. Though she kept back the part where she got to the corner of the street, sat there for a good hour before she went home, only to find nobody had even noticed she was gone.

'She told you she had a sore throat?' he asked, taking baby steps her way.

'She sure did.'

She bit her lip. Argh! Had she broken a confidence? No, she'd told Ruby she wouldn't tell her dad she was home from school, and that had been taken out of her hands by the nanny. Phew. She'd make sure the kid knew it the next time…

Only then did it hit Meg there wouldn't be a next time. She believed Zach wasn't kidding when he said he'd hired security to case the perimeter of the resort, so he'd probably already commissioned twenty-foot-high fences around the house as well.

If she were in Zach's shoes she'd keep his kid as far away from her as she possibly could.

Still, the thought of never seeing Ruby again made her heart give an all too familiar little twinge. But this wasn't about her. Then again, maybe, just maybe, as a nice little side effect, if she helped Zach get Ruby on track then she could stop those darned heart twinges for good.

He watched her with those clever dark eyes that made her feel as if she were melting from the inside out and he rowed.

She merely sat there and waited.

It paid off.

He took a deep breath, narrowed his eyes, then with all the enthusiasm of a man with a knife pressed to his ribs to make him talk, he said, 'She rang Felicia this morning, claiming a sore throat. Felicia called a cab to bring her home. When I heard my first thought was that it was a ruse. Then I wasn't sure. Do you think…?'

He shook his head and pressed the oars deeper into the water.

It more than paid off. Had Zach Jones just asked her for advice? She was shocked it had come so easily. But boy, was she ready to—

Who the heck was Felicia? Another woman in Zach's life? Meg wrapped her fingers around the bench to stop from tipping right off. 'Felicia is…?'

'The nanny.'

She all but laughed with relief. When Zach's eyes narrowed, she babbled, 'I had a nanny once. I told her I was adopted. She told a friend, who spilled the news to the press. Wow, I'd completely forgotten about that. Mum was so upset. And my father…' She shook her head to clear that image before the rest of the memory filtered through. 'Let's just say no more nannies came through the place.'

Zach's eyes widened a fraction. He really had no clue that young girls were as much about sugar and spice as they were about snakes and snails and puppy dogs' tails. It only made her more determined to make him see.

'Don't get me wrong. Other kids adored theirs,' she continued on. 'Tabitha still sends hers cards on Mother's Day. Does Ruby get on with Felicia?'

He waited a beat then nodded. 'She taught at Ruby's school for over twenty years. She's seen it all. I poached her earlier this year when Ruby came to live with me.'

'Well, that's great, then,' she said, her finger fiddling with her bottom lip as she frantically thought through what tack to take next. 'A girl needs firm boundaries as much as she needs her space.'

And then it hit her. Ruby hadn't always lived with him.

Where had she been? With her mother? Had they divorced? Had they never married? Had they been in love but couldn't live together? Was he still in love with her now? Was that where his innate darkness sprang from? There was no denying her heart hurt just thinking about it. It hurt for Zach. For Ruby. It was much easier letting it hurt for them than in any way for herself.

Now Meg needed to know the whole story so badly she could taste it. She held her breath.

'That's enough,' Zach said, and Meg's finger stilled. 'I have no idea how we started talking about this in the first place.'

Enough? They'd barely begun! She didn't have half the information she wanted—no, *required*—in order to help.

'You brought it up,' Meg shot back.

'I— What?' His oars paused mid-air.

'If you'd been sensible enough to ignore the fact that I happened upon your backyard, then we might never have had to have this conversation.'

'Why do I get the feeling you're used to getting your own way?' he growled.

'Ha! I have no idea because it certainly ain't true. I have three bossy older brothers and a father who thinks everything I do is a complete waste of time.'

Meg's eyes slammed shut and she bit her lip, but it was far too late. She'd said what she'd said. Somehow he'd done it again—given her all the rope she needed to hang herself.

She opened one eye to find him sitting ever so still, the oars resting lazily in their slips, dripping lake water over the bottom of the old wooden boat.

He was quiet for so long Meg could hear the sound of wings beating in the forest, the soft lapping of water against the side of the boat, and her own slow, deep breaths. Then he put the oars back where they were meant to be and pushed off.

He said, 'Ruby attends a local weekly boarding school.'

Meg could have kissed him. Right then and there. She had no clue why he'd let her off the hook when she'd been pressing herself into his personal life with barely concealed vigour. All she knew was that if he looked her in the eye rather than at some point over her shoulder she would probably have gone right ahead and kissed him.

'Where Felicia used to teach,' she encouraged, her voice soft, her words clearly thought out before she uttered a single word.

The muscle beneath his left eye twitched. Then as he pulled the oars through the water he said, 'It's barely a ten-minute drive from here. The same one she was attending before her mother passed away a few months ago.'

And there it was.

Meg's hands clasped one another so tight her fingers hurt. Ruby's mum had been gone only a few months. Oh, that poor little creature. No wonder he wanted to keep Ruby wrapped up in cotton wool. The fact she was able to go back to school at all was amazing. As for Zach…

She opened her mouth to ask how he was doing, when he cleared his throat and pushed the oars deeper into the water, sending them spearing back towards shore.

He said, 'This isn't the first time since she moved in with me that she's had a sore throat, a finger that twitches so hard she can't write, a foot so itchy she can't walk. So far all she's needed is a day at home and she's been right for another few weeks. So all in all I think we're doing okay.'

Doing okay? He cared. He considered. It was important to him to be a good father. In her humble opinion Zach was doing everything in his considerable power to do right by his little girl. And just like that all sorts of bone-deep, neglected, wishful, hopeful feelings beat to life inside her.

'Zach, I had no idea,' she said as she tried to

collect herself. 'Truly. I'm so sorry about your wife—'

He cut her off unceremoniously. 'Ruby's mother and I knew one another for a short time several years ago when I was visiting with a view to building this place. I didn't even know Ruby existed until after Isabel died.'

'So you weren't—'

So you're not still in love with her, was what she was trying not to ask.

'We weren't,' he said, insistent enough Meg had the feeling he'd heard all too clearly nonetheless. 'I was in Turkey when my lawyer contacted me with the news. After much legal wrangling I met a social worker here, at the house. And I met Ruby. She had one small suitcase and carried a teddy bear wearing a purple fairy dress under one skinny arm. I never expected her to be so small—'

Zach came to an abrupt halt, frowned deeply and glared down into his lap.

The backs of Meg's eyes burned. It took her a few moments to recognise it was the sharp sting of oncoming tears.

She never cried. Ever. Never sweated, never blushed, never cried. The moments she'd let herself succumb to her emotions were the times she'd been most deeply hurt—by careless whispers of envious types, by stories of horrendous depravity at the Valley Women's Shelter, even by herself. But this guy tugged shamelessly at hidden parts of her that didn't know the rules.

She blinked until the sensation went away.

'We're both trying to get used to our new living situation. To each other,' he went on, his voice raw, his eyes staring at some point on the bottom of the boat as it drifted steadily on. 'The last thing we need at this point is for her existence to come to the attention of the press. You obviously do know what they can be like. She needs to find her feet without constantly looking over her shoulder. She'll trip. She'll fall. She'll be hurt even more.'

He lifted his dark eyes to hers. There was a newfound lightness within them that came with getting everything off his chest. But the second he remembered he'd been divulging his story to her, it was gone.

'Meg,' he said, his voice rough, beseeching.

She breathed deep to calm her thundering heart and said, 'I know I haven't done much to make you believe this, but you really can trust me. I'm exceptionally good at keeping secrets. You have no idea how good, which only proves my point. I'll not breathe a word.'

'I truly hope so.'

She smiled. He managed to do a shadow of the same. And in that moment of silent communion something rare and magical was forged between them.

It felt a lot like trust.

CHAPTER SIX

THE boat bumped against solid ground.

Meg flinched, her flat shoes slipping on the wet wood, but she caught herself in time. She'd been so engrossed in Zach, in his story, in the man, she hadn't even noticed the head-high reeds encroaching.

Zach tied them off. He threw the cooler onto the wooden deck, then leaned over and held out a hand.

She took it, the loaded silence of the lingering moment of amity still making her feel all floaty and surreal.

Once on the jetty she took off his hat, ran a quick hand through her messy curls and handed it to him along with his blanket. He wrapped his hands around both, but didn't tug. Meg looked up into his dark eyes.

Her heart felt heavy in her chest. Her body felt heavy on her legs. The only thing about her that felt light was her head. Which was probably why she said, 'Now that I know everything there is to know about you, are you finally going to give in and stop stalking me?'

His dark brows rose. His voice, on the other hand, deepened. 'Is that what I've been doing?'

She said, 'Either that or fifty acres *really* isn't quite as much room as it sounds.'

From nowhere his head rocked back and he laughed. The sexy sound reverberated deep in her stomach, leaving it feeling hollow. As it faded to a smile in his eyes it left a new kind of warmth in its place she wasn't sure what to do with.

'I like you better this way,' she admitted.

'What way?'

'Not bossing me around. You should try that more.'

He gave the blanket and hat a tug. She shuffled forward a step before letting go and he threw them lazily onto the cooler.

He looked back at her. The earlier glints in his dark eyes had been mere imitations of the glints glinting at her now. The kind of glints she now wished she'd not wished for. They were dazzling, they were blistering, they were completely incapacitating.

His voice rumbled, low and deep. 'By that logic if I continue that way you'll only like me more.'

'You can't argue with logic,' she said, trying to sound pithy; instead she sounded as if she was flirting. Which, of course, she was.

How could she not? He was glinting and smiling, and somehow, whether by her brilliant psychological tactics or by his choice alone, she'd been allowed to see a little of the man behind the mask.

What she saw there she liked.

And by the look in his eyes what he saw in front of him right at this moment he liked right back.

Meg licked her lips. His hot gaze trailed slowly down the curves of her face until it landed square upon her mouth. His eyes turned dark as night and he breathed out. Hard.

Despite knowing that what was about to happen was reckless and pointless and born of nothing more concrete than the ephemeral connection of confidences shared, Meg just stood there, her entire body vibrating in anticipation.

Zach slid his arm gently around her back, with such little pressure she had time and room to curl away.

She knew she should. She thought to the very last she would. She was *always* the one to back away first before anything truly serious came to bear. But her toes curled into her shoes and she held her ground.

Zach's brow creased for the briefest of seconds as though he was surprising even himself before a small smile eased onto his mouth. Hers lifted in its image.

Then he pulled her in close. The warmth of his sun-drenched body pressed through her dress until every inch of skin, exposed and concealed, felt as if it had begun to glow.

Her hand fluttered up to rest against his chest to find it hard, fit, unyielding, everything she'd thought him to be. Only now she knew that beneath the tough exterior beat the heart of a man whose primary goal was the protection of a little girl.

He leaned down and moved his lips over hers. He tasted like chocolate muffins. She was toast.

The kiss was slow. Dreamy. As if he had no intention of missing out on experiencing every single nuance.

It took about three and a half seconds before Meg slid her arms around his neck and pressed up onto her toes to get closer to him. Sinking against him. Soaking up every bit of him that she possibly could.

With a groan that reverberated through her body like a little earthquake, his strong arms wrapped so tight around her he lifted her off the jetty as though she weighed nothing at all.

The kiss deepened. And deepened again.

His tongue eased into her mouth, caressing the edges of her teeth, sliding over the tiny chip in her front tooth, sending delicious shivers through her, touching her tongue for the briefest of moments before it was gone.

She was breathless and hot. Her skin hummed. Her insides ached. Her toes curled. Her lungs burned. And the kiss continued as beautifully indulgent and unhurried as it had begun.

Until her flat shoes slid from her feet, landing on the jetty with a soft slap, leaving her feet bare, and leaving her feeling exposed. Completely at his mercy. And finally her senses came swarming back.

She pulled away. Ever so slightly. But he felt it. Slowly, gently, he placed her back on the jetty. And they uncurled their limbs from around one another.

Only once there was enough space for a summer breeze to slide between them did Zach say, 'I'm not sure where that came from.'

'I am,' she said, her cheeks pinking the second the words left her mouth. But it was the truth. She'd wanted to do that since the moment she'd first seen him.

It got her a slow, easy smile and a nod. The moment of accord, of finally admitting to each other what they both felt, was even more formidable than the kiss itself.

'I'd better go,' she said. 'My posse will be moseying back to camp any time soon.'

She reached out and rested her hand on his arm. His skin was so warm, the energy coursing through him so vital, her heart rate rose in direct response.

'I'm really sorry about Isabel,' she said.

His mouth quirked, but he didn't smile. And she wondered if he'd been hoping the kiss would wipe everything else from her mind. She wasn't about to tell him how close it had come.

Instead, she squeezed his arm again, and said,

'But I'm not worried about Ruby. I have no doubt she's in good hands. She's really lucky to have you.'

She lifted her hand in a small wave, then gathered her shoes and jogged up the jetty, her mind already playing over the fib she'd have to create for Rylie and Tabitha to explain where she'd been, what she'd been doing, and why she was floating an inch off the ground but couldn't quite remove the frown from her forehead at the same time.

Later that night, once Rylie and Tabitha were snoring lightly in their rooms Meg lay on her bed, wide-awake, her mobile phone warm in her palms.

She'd been tossing it from hand to hand for a good couple of hours, ever since she'd got off the phone from saying goodnight to Olivia and Violet, Brendan's girls.

They'd sounded bright, cheery, happy. What had she expected? They were seven and four, and they had ponies, ballet lessons, piano, rock climbing, Chinese and French lessons, summer trips around the world with their grandmother, twenty-year-old nannies who spoilt them rotten, and a dad who clearly wrestled with the amount of time he spent at work while they grew up without him there to see it.

But as she lay back on her bed, the pale summer moon spilling light through the far window creating a hypnotic play of light and shadow on the ceiling, the fairy dust cleared from her eyes and Ruby's small face looked back at her instead.

She'd seen so much of herself in the kid's mutinous streak. That spark could be so easily deflated. Or worse, it could spin out of control. She hoped not. With all her might. Not just for Ruby. But also for Zach.

Big, bad, daunting, noble, solid Zach Jones.

Growing up in her family, the only kind of masculine strength she'd understood till she met him had been overt. Overpowering. Uncompromising.

Zach's strength came from somewhere much deeper. A place he didn't feel compelled to proclaim to the world. The fact that she'd been allowed to witness it in the revelation of how he'd changed his life for his little girl made it that much more compelling. It was like seeing a fireman rescue a kitten from a tree.

She'd hate to see all his good work go to waste. But since Zach's parenting skills were now obviously nothing like her father's, Ruby might not need the intervention her adolescent mutiny necessitated after all. She struggled with deciding what to do.

One thing she knew had been a bad decision on both their parts had been that kiss.

Her fingers lifted to stroke her lips as they must have done a few dozen times that afternoon. She could still taste his sweetness, sense his warmth all around her, feel his hardness imprinted on every inch of her body as if it had happened mere moments ago.

Soft, dreamy, luxurious, deep, unguarded, magic.

And indefensible. Because Zach Jones had a child.

When she'd ruled out any chance of having kids of her own, kids who—just because they were hers—would never live up to her father's expectations of them, it had never occurred to her that she might one day meet a man who came with kids of his own. Her usual types were never that proactive.

Then Zach had to come stomping into her life, shaking loose old choices she'd never thought she'd have to revisit again.

But no. Her nieces were living proof of why she'd done the right thing.

They seemed fine, now. But they were little kids. They ought to wear gumboots and get into mud-pie fights, not wear dresses and tights and patent leather shoes when playing in the backyard.

The pressure for them to live up to her father's unwavering ideal of what a Kelly had to be was mounting. And soon they'd be old enough to feel it. Soon they'd be old enough to know.

There was no way she'd wish that pressure on any child. Not by blood, and not by association. Because she knew the consequences.

She threw her phone across the room and it landed with a thud on a couch in the corner.

She tried humming Stevie Wonder to clear her

head, but it didn't work. Zach's deep voice rang louder still.

She liked the guy. She adored how he kissed. She was smitten with his efforts to do right by Ruby. And she was in his debt for letting her get away with the unforgivable slip about her exceedingly private dealings with her father.

But she wasn't any good for him any more than he would be good for her. He might not see it yet, but he had the natural inclination to be some kind of dad. He'd want more kids down the line, and with her insides the way they were she could never give them to him.

Meg turned on her side, tucked her thighs against her belly, and slid her hands beneath her pillow. The sheer curtains over the ceiling–to-floor windows— chosen especially to *not* let a girl sleep in when there was jogging to be done—flapped under the soft push of air-conditioned air.

Out there, in that big, rambling, amazing house of his, Zach would soon be asleep. She wondered if he dreamt. What he dreamt about. And more importantly, who.

It had long since been dark by the time Zach stepped foot in the place he'd called home for the past few months. He was humming as he shut the front door. It took a few moments until he realised it was KC and the Sunshine Band. Classic disco.

Throwing a full set of keys onto the sideboard rather than a simple hotel card still felt strange.

Being shuffled from foster home to state institution and back again, he'd hit a point where he'd simply stopped feeling connected to places, to possessions, to people. Living in this large, rambling house, sleeping in the same bed every night, seeing the same faces every day, he felt the return of the natural desire to preserve those connections. Along with that came the niggling fear that it all might yet be taken away.

'Good evening, Zach,' a voice called out to him in the darkness.

He jumped. 'Felicia. You took a year off my life.'

'Working to all hours will do that to you far more quickly,' Ruby's nanny said. 'I'd say you are a prime candidate for attending one of those wellness programmes that are so trendy nowadays.'

Zach gave her shadowy figure a flat stare. 'If I'd known you had such a funny bone I'd have left you in that draughty old school.'

The older woman patted him on the arm.

He glanced down the dark front hallway towards the bright haven of the warm family kitchen, his nose catching the delicious concoction of homey smells that meant there were leftovers waiting for him in the oven. 'Is she still awake?'

He felt her shake her head. 'Out like a light the minute her head hit the pillow.'

'Have you heard any—?' He stopped, hoping he wouldn't have to put into words the wretched sounds she screamed out every few nights.

'Not a peep. What with her sore throat I'd say she needed the rest.' She tossed her large book bag over her shoulder. 'Goodnight, then. I'll see you in the morning.'

He heard her meet up with one of the rotation of night staff who escorted her back to her own bungalow down the way, their voices trailing into the distance until he was left with silence.

Rather than heading for the beguiling scent of zucchini quiche he took a left. The light from the kitchen faded the farther he moved through the house.

He reached Ruby's bedroom door and stared at her name spelled out in big pink letters, his ears straining to hear the sound of her sleeping breaths.

He could have been home hours earlier. Certainly before her bedtime. Instead he'd remained shackled to his workstation in the Blueberry Ash Bungalow he'd taken as his office, telling himself Ruby wouldn't have expected him home as it was still officially a school night. The truth was the thought of having to question her, to chastise her even, for skipping school had left him in a cold sweat.

She was seven, for Pete's sake. He was thirty-five and operated a massive multinational company. There wasn't anyone on earth who had a hope in hell of intimidating him. Yet from the day he'd first looked into those all too intelligent brown eyes he'd lived with the fear that, though he'd *never* abandon her, there was always the chance she'd decide she did not want him.

He ran a hand over his face, the pads of his fingers rasping against the day-old shave, before resting his palm on the cool wood of her bedroom door.

The instinct to press open the door, sneak in and check on his daughter, to let himself believe she slept because *he'd* made her feel safe, was so strong. Yet every night he managed to talk himself out of it.

He might wake her. She might see him and expect her mum and become distressed. He might get used to her being there.

Yet this night the urge felt different. Not nearly so complicated. Today his knowledge of what a girl needed in order to feel safe had been increased tenfold in one short conversation with the most unlikely source—Meg Kelly.

She'd been so confident that Ruby needed her space. And just as sure that it was okay for him to impulsively not want to give it to her. And even more than okay that Ruby knew it. His instincts were spot on. Maybe he did have it within him to do this right after all.

He wrapped his hand around the door handle.

Good hands, Meg had called them, and with enough vehemence he'd let himself believe it too.

He went in. Even in the darkness there was no mistaking the big white bed jutting out into the centre of the largest bedroom in the house. He might have gone overboard with the rocking horse, the padded window seat, the library stacked with *Saddle Club* books, the tea-party table, the twenty different dolls, but he'd taken note of every lick of advice from Felicia and her other teachers who'd known her the past couple of years and let his International Resort Decorator go crazy, no expenses spared.

He took a few steps into the plush-carpeted room until moonlight spilling through the faraway window gave him enough light to see that beneath the pink-and-white lacy bedcovers lay a skinny, young girl.

A handful of days had passed since she'd been home for the weekend, but he was sure she'd grown. Her dark hair splayed across her pillow with such perfection it was as though someone had brushed out every strand. Her face was smooth and unlined. Her breathing even and unworried. Her throat not bothering her a bit.

Before he knew it was coming he smiled wide. Cheeky kid. She even had her nanny fooled. But Meg, considering her more recent experience being a daughter, had seen through the subterfuge in a second.

He took another step closer until he was near

enough he allowed himself the small gesture of wiping a long, straight lock of hair from across her eyes.

Ruby stirred. Mumbled a bit. He froze. But she soon resettled—taking up the whole bed, one arm flung over her head. Exactly the way he'd always slept.

His heart slammed against his ribs. This creature was his daughter. His responsibility. His only family. If anyone did anything, said anything, printed anything that made the authorities even *think* about denying her to him…

Before his throat clogged so tight he couldn't breathe he spun on his heel and walked from the room.

'Daddy?' a soft voice called when he was a metre away from being home free.

He turned; Ruby was sitting up, a shadow in the darkness, as he must have been to her. He found his voice for her. 'Yes, honey?'

'Nothing. Just checking.'

Checking to see he was real.

Checking to see he was still around.

Checking to see he hadn't disappeared right when she was getting used to him being there. God, how he knew that feeling. That loathsome, sinking, hollowness when someone you trusted to love you left without looking back.

'I'm here,' he said, his voice gruff. 'I'm not going anywhere. You can go back to sleep.'

By the slow, even breaths coming from her bed, he knew she already was.

He closed her door and paced into the kitchen where he leant his hands on the island bench in the middle of the huge room.

Felicia had left out his newspapers. Beside them sat a permission slip from Ruby's school for an upcoming field trip, and a spaghetti jar overfilled with a mishmash of local wildflowers. He imagined Ruby picking them for Felicia as an act of contrition, and Felicia falling for the sore-throat stunt all the harder. Smart kid.

He played with the rubbery, cream petal of a waxflower. Working in solitary, coming home late to a dark house, eating leftovers, keeping his weekends completely free to spend them at Ruby's beck and call within the confines of a handful of safe places; this was the inflexible life he'd chosen. This was how things were going to be for the next dozen-odd years. No more hands-on business, no more travel, no more adult company?

Meg Kelly's lovely face swam all too easily back into his mind.

For the first time since he'd set foot in the door—but certainly not the first time that day— he remembered the kiss. God, the delights he'd found within that mouth. It had drawn him in like a siren song he could no longer resist. But her warm skin, and her goddess curves and her instant response had made it impossible for him to tear himself away.

He pushed away from the island and moved to the oven to grab his dinner. Oven mitts the last thing on his mind, the ceramic quiche tray burnt his fingers. He let go and it smashed to the floor. Egg and zucchini and cheese flew everywhere, splattering the wooden cupboards and embedding themselves in every bit of slate-tile grout it could find.

He swore at the great mess profusely but sotto voce, always remembering Ruby was asleep down the hall. He flipped on the tap and shoved his stinging fingers beneath the cold-water stream.

What the hell was he thinking? Kissing Meg. Confiding in her. Her pretty words might have sounded believable at the time, but Meg Kelly could yet bring down his carefully balanced house of cards with one word whispered in the wrong direction. Her best friend was a journalist, for Pete's sake! Dammit. That mouth of hers could prove to be his downfall in more ways than one.

He turned off the tap, wiped his hands down his trousers when he couldn't find a handy tea towel, and set to cleaning up the mess.

After cheese on toast for dinner he signed Ruby's permission slip with a flourish so fierce he tore the paper.

He'd let himself be wrapped around a female finger for the last time. The next time Ruby tried to pull a stunt like skipping school, he *would* talk with her. He would grow some backbone and set some boundaries.

Apparently boundaries were something young girls needed. Or so some would have him believe.

CHAPTER SEVEN

IN LIEU of the dawn jog, the next morning Meg slid notes beneath the girls' doors saying she was taking the hike through the national forest instead and to meet her at the rendezvous point at seven.

After finally falling asleep some time after two she needed the extra hour to recuperate. But that wasn't why hiking was suddenly her new favourite pastime.

She was avoiding Zach.

After the dreams she'd had, G-rated dreams of white picket fences and yellow Labrador puppies with herself in an apron washing dishes while looking out a kitchen window at a yard full of kids, she needed to put as much of the fifty acres of resort land between her and Zach Jones as she could.

She stood at the back of the thankfully large hiking group, decked out in what seemed the most appropriate hiking attire she had, twisting her crazy morning hair into two thick plaits, determined not to let the humidity beat her, ready to put aside the past couple of days and start her holiday anew.

'Good morning,' a deep voice rumbled beside her.

She snapped her eyes shut, not needing to look up to know who the voice belonged to. That tone alone could make her skin hum no matter what it said.

'So where are the other two musketeers this fine morning?' he asked.

Thankful for the excuse not to look him in the eye, she glanced over her shoulder to find the path behind her empty. She said, 'Still snug in their warm beds, I expect. Who knew I'd turn out to be the energetic one?'

Who knew? They knew. And that was why they weren't coming. Oh, no...

In an effort to be honest with her best friends while still keeping from them everything she was unable—or not yet ready—to share, she'd been brief when mentioning her run-ins with Zach. Obviously too brief. Her insouciance hadn't fooled them for a single second. They knew something was up, and being her best friends they'd optimistically assumed her reticence meant true romance was in the air. They were leaving her alone so that it might flourish.

Being stuck with Zach looking all scruffy and gorgeous, with no buffer to keep her out of harm's way, was all she deserved.

She tied off her second plait then glanced at him causally from the corner of her eye, catching sight of yet more cargo pants, yet another sexily faded T-shirt, a tattered old backpack snugly attached to his back and the same well-worn cap she'd seen him wear before.

Her perusal ground to a halt when it reached his mouth. Her own turned as dry as dust as their kiss came rushing back to her in Technicolor. She licked her lips, then croaked, 'Please don't tell me I've accidentally done something else that would necessitate you tailing me?'

'Now what could possibly make you think my presence here has anything to do with you?'

Before she could come up with a succinct retort, the wellness facilitator called out, 'Today the crew heading up our new St Barts resort are joining us to see how we Aussies do it. So let's lift our feet, keep up a super pace, and ooh and ahh at the local flora and fauna like we've never seen anything so fabulous!'

'You're here to train your next crew?' she said, mostly to herself.

'Beautiful *and* brainy. Who knew?'

Zach tugged on one of her plaits, shot her a grin that was complete with the glint that made her common sense unceasingly fall to pieces, pulled his cap lower over his face then jogged ahead.

With the words *beautiful and brainy* ringing in

her ears, she stared at his back until he was swallowed by the forest.

Amazing. He was well over six feet tall, with skin like bronze and the build of a world-class athlete, yet he clearly had no clue *that* was why half the people in the group would be wondering who he was. It wouldn't matter if she was sitting in his lap or a million miles away.

Meg hitched her shiny new Juniper Falls backpack into a more comfy position on her shoulders, took one last glance back at the empty path, then followed on as the group turned off the running track.

They soon found a network of wide wooden walkways with the kind of gentle slope built to accommodate every level of trail rambler and Meg was truly surprised to soon find herself contentedly lost in the rhythmic pace of her feet.

Before long they were ushered through a gap in the railing as they headed off the main tourist trail. The path became instantly less clear-cut, less regularly tramped, and the gentle path gave way to one in which they had to walk single file, at times grasping at vines to pull themselves up the face of a steep rise.

Sweat dripped down the sides of Meg's face, down her spine and behind her knees. She could feel spirals of her hair plastered against her cheeks and the back of her neck. When she licked her lips she could taste salt. She gave up trying to hear the guide over her laboured breathing and just climbed.

Meg wasn't sure if she'd picked up her pace or Zach had slowed, but somehow right when she needed leverage to step over a particularly slippery-looking rock as she picked a path across a slow-moving stream, his hand was there to help her leap across to the opposite bank.

'Thanks,' she said, her voice rough from lack of use. 'Are we there yet?'

From her view of his profile she caught his smile, this one complete with eye crinkles. Her heart skipped a beat, which, considering her fitness level and the uneven ground, was not smart.

'Not far now,' he said, his voice as clear as if he'd been standing still the past half-hour.

'If I have a complaint do I really have to write to management?'

'Hit me. I can take it.'

'Are the super-early starts entirely necessary?'

The smile spread to laughter as though it was the most natural thing for him to do. 'The days get hot very quickly around here.'

'I'm not sure I believe that makes a lick of difference to your sadistic timetable planners.'

The eye crinkles deepened. 'That's because you're too smart for your own good.'

'Mmm. So does that mean you actually believe in the stuff you're spouting? Inner health, inner happiness and all that.'

His eye crinkles faded as he gave her question

consideration. The guy listened, seriously listened, to what she had to say. Most men in his position patted her on the head as if she were a clever puppy before deferring to her brothers, not caring that she might be a woman with ideas and opinions and more street smarts than they had in their little fingers. No wonder she was finding it harder and harder to pull herself away from this one.

He said, 'I believe that what you put into your life is what you get out of it. Treat it well, it'll treat you well. Surround yourself only with positive people and they'll affect your life positively. Fill your body and your mind with rubbish and rubbish is all you can ever hope to be.'

Meg let those pearls sink in and then kind of wished she hadn't asked. Because it shed a new light on how she must have appeared to others. And to him.

She attended parties to keep her profile current, so that meant she was a party girl. Nothing deeper. Nothing more. And it was entirely her own doing.

She kept hush-hush the best parts of herself; the truth about the number of women at the Valley Women's Shelter she'd secretly helped over the years. That way *nobody* knew the real her. Not her family. Not even her friends.

For years she'd thought she had the best of both worlds—public affection and private fulfilment. But Zach's words made her wish *someone* knew.

They made her wish he knew. The urge to just blurt it all out then and there was a powerful thing.

But then what? He was too perceptive. He'd wonder why she needed to spend time with battered women and displaced children in particular, and why she'd even hidden the fact in the first place.

Nah. Better to keep things as they were. Best not to discover people might only be attracted to the light, bright, amusing, easily palatable version of herself. Zach included. She wasn't sure she was prepared to know the answer to that one.

Realising the silence was stretching on far too long, she forced a dazzling party-girl smile and said, 'So you are what you eat?'

His cheek lifted. 'In not so many words.'

'By that logic if I go home right now and marinate myself in chocolate and red wine, then at the very least I'll die tasty.'

He laughed softly, before saying, 'You can't argue with logic.'

Meg's breath caught in her throat. He'd just had to go and use the last words she'd said to him before they'd kissed, hadn't he? Her heart beat double time. She breathed deep to control it before she keeled over.

Perhaps he hadn't realised what he'd said, because he just turned and followed the group. Or perhaps the kiss hadn't affected him nearly as much as it had affected her.

Good, she thought. *Fantastic even. Fan-bloody-tastic.*

Now they were descending again. Single file. Meg was caught behind Zach, so naturally while she ought to have been watching her feet she watched him instead. The spring of curls against his tanned neck. The athletic ease with which he strode the trail.

Surely he'd felt *something* when they'd kissed. She'd felt magic.

When her foot half missed a stepping stone, she stumbled and caught hold of his backpack for support.

'You okay back there?' he asked, snapping a hand behind him to cradle her hip.

She closed her eyes against the flow of feeling rushing through her that felt more tangible and immediate than mere magic. 'Mostly.'

'Take my shoulders.'

'Why?' she asked.

He glanced up at her, his dark eyes shadowed beneath his cap. And she was certain his voice dropped a note or two when he said, 'Because it only gets riskier from here.'

'I'll be fine,' she said, her voice husky.

'Meg—'

'I'm not completely inept, you know. I may not know which direction I'm heading, but I can put one foot in front of the other without falling flat on my face.' *Most of the time.* 'I can do this on my own.'

Ignoring her outburst, Zach simply took her by the waist and physically lifted her and placed her to the left of the path so that those behind her could get past.

Once they were alone with their group bundling down the descent in front of them, Zach said, 'Relax, Meg. I'm not offering you anything more than a hand down the mountain.'

Meg swallowed, the lack of saliva making her throat scratch so she winced. His dark eyes slid down her face to rest on her lips. His grip tightened. Infinitesimally. And she felt in his touch the same confusion of want and restraint surging through her body.

Triumph coursed through her. He'd felt every bit of enchantment in that kiss that she had.

Triumph fast turned to confusion. What was she meant to do with the knowledge that helping her down the hill wasn't all he wanted to give her any more than that was all she wanted from him?

In the quiet that followed Meg realised the group had moved far enough away that birdsong came back to the forest. The water in the stream they had crossed bubbled melodiously about the fall of rocks unable to completely block its path.

They were to all intents and purposes alone. Anything could happen. Like having photos of 'Meg Kelly and friend' getting up to no good being splashed all over the Internet within hours. For that he'd never forgive her.

She took his hands from her and pressed them back to his sides. 'Thanks for the offer, but I just slipped a little on some moss. I'll pay more attention to where I put my feet.'

His eyes finally, thankfully, skimmed from her mouth back to her eyes and his hands moved to grip the straps of his backpack. 'Just be careful, for my sake. I don't need you slipping and breaking a bone.'

'God, no. The press would be all over this place like a rash. Which is, of course, the last thing we want.'

'We want?'

'Yes, *we*. As in we agree that it's Ruby who's front and foremost in our minds when we happen upon one another.'

Ruby who should be reason enough we never happen upon one another again.

After one final dark glance he nodded, then turned and headed down the ragged path.

'Keep up,' he called without turning, 'before we have to send out a search party for you again.'

'A search party? Please,' she called back as she walked unsteadily down the trail.

Had he just said 'again'?

Five long, hot minutes later, the descent evened out and the path became made up of wide, neat steps carved into layers of grey rock.

The group spread out, walking in clumps. The scurrying, flapping, whistling noises of the forest had been overtaken by the nearby sound of rushing water. The overgrown forest cleared to reveal a vertical slant of wet rock that was so high Meg had to crane her neck to see the sliver of sunlight above.

'Hold onto the handrails, step carefully, and prepare yourselves for something fabulous!' the guide called out.

Meg followed Zach into a gap in the rock. And darkness. And sudden dank coolness. The sweat covering her whole body brought her skin up in goose bumps.

Bit by bit, step by slow step, Meg's eyes became used to the gloom. Up ahead, through the bobbing heads of her fellow hikers, there was light. Eerie, green light.

Then suddenly she stepped onto the edge of a high-domed cave. At her feet lapped a pool of bright green water clear enough to see the floor was made of a tumble of smooth stones of all shapes and sizes. Above, through a gap way up high in the ceiling, a stunning, glowing, white sheet of water splashed magnificently into the deep centre of the pool. It was literally one of the most beautiful things she'd ever seen.

'I give you Juniper Falls,' Zach said from somewhere to her right.

Meg couldn't think of a thing to say back. She

just let it wash over her—the noise, the colour, the primal violence and beauty of it all.

'Worth the early start?' Zach asked some time later.

'And then some,' she said, drawing her eyes away from the spectacle to give him a quick smile.

A couple of nearby camera flashes went off. She took a step away from him, her eyes instantly scanning the crowd for the offender. But everyone was ogling the waterfall, not their blurry shapes in the semi-darkness.

'Photos don't do it justice,' he said. 'Just look, listen, absorb, get your fill. You won't forget. This moment will be with you for ever.'

While Zach kept his gaze dead ahead, and despite the splendour raging in front of her, Meg's remained locked on him.

As though he knew just what she was taking her fill of, he turned to look at her. His brows came together and his right cheek creased into a sexy arch, questioning her. She shook her head, shrugged. What could she possibly say?

His eyes left hers to rove slowly over her face as though he too was taking the chance to memorise every centimetre.

He was right—it was a moment she knew she would never forget.

The group spread out, some continuing around the other side of the pool, others finding patches of sunshine so they could sit and relax. A few game souls took off their shoes and waded into the shallows.

'Coming?' he asked, holding out a hand.

'How about you point the way to the best spot, then you can get back to work?'

His eyes narrowed, then he looked about and saw the camera flashes for what they potentially were. He took a slow step away from her. And even though she'd been the one to encourage the move, her heart clenched just a little in her chest.

He curled his hand back to his side as he pulled his old hat farther down over his eyes. Then he gave her a long, straight look. 'As it turns out I have a little time to spare for my guests if you'd care to follow me.'

She swallowed and nodded. Then followed him to a large, mostly dry rock on which sunshine dappled through the ferns above. Meg settled herself onto it with a thankful sigh.

'Is the water warm?' she asked.

He stood, towering over her. 'See for yourself.'

When she leant over and whisked her hand through the clear water the illusion firmed. It was warm enough to swim in, but cool enough to soothe her hot hands.

Zach filled his flask with water, then his tanned throat worked hard as he chugged it down. When Zach saw her eyeing his drink bottle with her tongue practically hanging out of her mouth he handed it to her.

Her lips hovered where his lips had been. She imagined she could smell chocolate muffins. She closed her eyes, all but groaning as the blissfully cool liquid slid down her scorching throat.

Zach's voice was loud enough for those nearest to hear when he went all 'tour guide' on her and said, 'The pool is fed by the falls and the overflow creates an underwater spring to the south, which feeds into a stream that heads off into the national park. With the constant pummelling, the floor at the centre of the pool is the softest sand you'll ever feel.'

She put the lid back on his flask and handed it to him, their fingers sliding past one another as they exchanged the bottle from her hot hand to his.

'So you've swum here?' she asked, looking back out into the pool, tucking her shaking hand tight into her lap.

'Once or twice.'

'I can't imagine when you'd find the time. What with running a trillion businesses and looking after you know who.'

She felt him draw back. She'd been discreet. But it hadn't mattered. The withdrawal of all that lovely warmth stung.

And shocked her sensible. Even though they were both on the same side in wanting to protect his daughter, while it was her wish, it was his mission in life.

She slung her backpack onto the rock between them, the most substantial wall she could mount on short notice, then said, 'I'm sorry. I won't bring that subject up again.'

His voice was low and intimate when he said, 'Meg, I wanted to—'

She flapped a hand between them. 'It's fine. I understand.'

'No, I don't think you do,' he said. 'I wanted to tell you… She made me pancakes.'

Meg's eyes slid to his, envy and delight spilling through her in tandem. 'She did? When?'

'This morning. Before she went back to school.'

'Jeez, she's an early riser. Like father like daughter, I guess.'

He glanced at her with an expression she'd never seen on him before. As if he'd thought the same, but couldn't be convinced that it wasn't just wishful thinking. It got to her, like an arrow straight to the heart.

'Were they any good?' she asked, her voice reed-thin. 'The pancakes.'

'Atrocious.' He laughed softly.

'But you ate them all,' she said, knowing the answer before she even asked the question.

He nodded once. 'I certainly did.'

The arrow in her heart stabbed a little deeper.

She tried to imagine her own father eating pancakes she'd made. Unless they'd been fit for the table of literal kings he would have taken one look and fed them to the dogs. And he would somehow have made sure she knew it too.

She swallowed down the heady mix of new good and old bad feelings rising far too quickly inside her.

'She asked after you, you know,' Zach said, glancing away from her to stare out at some vague spot in the distance.

Meg raised her eyes to the roof of the cave to hold back the encroaching sting. If he knew what was good for him, the guy should really stop talking. Now.

She knew what was good for her and still asked, 'What did she say?'

'Young girls need their mystery. Or so I've been told.'

'Hey now,' she laughed, taking a quick moment to brush a finger under her eyes, 'that's not fair. I was being nice giving you all that secret girls' business insight, and now you're using it against me.'

'Fair enough,' he said, 'then I will tell you that it was something you said to her yesterday that had her heading off to school today like she had the wind at her heels. So thank you for that too.'

Wow. She'd done that? She gave him a nod. It was either that or croak out, *You're welcome*.

'Mr Jones,' a woman's voice with a lilting foreign accent said from between them.

Meg flinched and dragged herself out of the cloud of intimacy that had wrapped itself around them like a slow, thick, enshrouding fog shifting across the pool.

She turned to find a stunning redhead, her hair neat as a pin, her Juniper Falls uniform pressed, not a lick of sweat anywhere. Meg ran a quick hand over her fuzzy plaits and so wished she hadn't. It would have been better not to know.

'Claudia,' Zach said, his voice so cool and aloof Meg was surprised to remember when he'd last used that tone of voice with her. 'What can I do for you?'

'Sorry to interrupt, but the St Barts group had a few questions about the morning they wanted to run by you while we had a moment's respite.'

'Of course. Claudia, this is Meg, a guest at the resort. Meg, Claudia will be my St Barts manager,' he explained.

'St Barts? You lucky duck,' Meg said with the instant return of her practised smile. 'And thank you, Zach, for taking the time to explain how the waterfall works. It was most informative.'

Claudia gave her a short smile, then headed off to join the St Barts crew.

Zach looked across at her with a kind of smile she was having more and more trouble resisting. 'Most informative?'

'Well,' she said, 'it was.'

Zach stood, yet he lingered.

'Go,' she said, shooing him away. 'Please. I'm not

going to fall into the pool and drown and cause you endless hassles. I promise.'

His brow furrowed, then he said, 'No, that's not…I was going to ask if I'll see you tonight.'

'Tonight?' Her heart beat so hard in her throat she was certain it must have been obvious to everyone in sight.

'You are coming to the luau, are you not?'

'The what?'

'There's a clearing at the west corner of the lake on which we've created a beach. The staff put on a controlled bonfire there once a week. Have you even read the brochure?'

'I glanced at it. Briefly.' Trying to find chocolate, trying to find the Wellness Building. Both times she'd only found more of him. 'Look, I'm not sure what our plans are for tonight—'

'The St Barts team will be there tonight so I was thinking about putting in an appearance. For their sake,' he said. Adding, 'There'll be marshmallows.'

She couldn't help herself. She licked her lips.

And he laughed. Throaty, loud laughter that resonated through her bones as though her marrow were a twanged guitar string.

'Real marshmallows?' she asked, her voice comically low, amazed at the cool she could still find within herself when she needed it most. Thank heavens for her years of training. 'Or soy-based, gluten-free, sugar-free sticky balls?'

'Real marshmallows. Bags and bags of them. Pink and white. Sticks supplied if you're a toaster.'

'Sure I'm a toaster. You?'

'All the way. But just in case you need something to keep you going until then...' He tossed her a small package wrapped in the ubiquitous Juniper Falls pale green. He tipped his cap at her, then bounded across the rocks to join the St Barts crew.

Meg tore it open to find herself holding a small packet of M&Ms. She laughed out loud, then pressed her finger to her mouth before her fellow hikers discovered her laughing to herself and realised they ought to have been paying more heed to the frizzy brunette in their midst.

CHAPTER EIGHT

ZACH stood on a corner of the lake's beach not lit by the blazing fire, feet bare as the day he was born, dressed top to toe in linen he'd ironed himself, and a hot pink lei someone he didn't recognise had thrown over his head.

'You're a fool,' he muttered to himself for about the seventh time in the past ten minutes. 'You and Ruby might have had a good morning because of something *she* said, and maybe you can't get that kiss out of your mind, but by poking your head out of your perfectly adequate cave again and again just to get another glimpse makes you a damn fool.'

His hands gripped the lei, crushing the flowers, but before he had the chance to whip it over his neck the sound of female laughter split the night.

Glitter twinkled in the darkness. Three distinct voices wafted towards him, followed by three female forms. The other two must have been her friends. All he saw was Meg.

Her dark hair had been pulled back into a slick ponytail. Huge hooped earrings hung from her ears to her shoulders, encrusted with more diamond dust than most women would ever own. But it was the dress that had him clenching his fingers into his palms.

Fire-engine red it was, made of some sparkly material that clung to her torso like second skin, cinching tight at her waist then billowing all the way to her ankles. Her shoulders were bare, her décolletage on display within a deep V, and around the middle she was tied up with a big red bow.

Never had he been given a gift quite like that. He'd obviously kept the wrong friends.

She leaned in as a staff member explained the 'no shoes on the beach policy' for the luau, and without hesitation she rested her elbow on someone's shoulder, hitched her voluminous skirt as high as her knee and proceeded to uncurl a good metre of red leather strap wound about her calf.

Zach closed his eyes and prayed for mercy.

When he opened them it was to see Meg, barefoot, bouncing onto the sand with the exuberance of a puppy. Mid-twirl he got a load of the back of the dress—she was completely bare from a small clip at the back of her neck all the way to her waist. It wasn't quite low enough to give him a glimpse of the tattoo he knew was there, but low enough he ran a hand hard over his mouth.

He knew what it was about her that had him

tempting fate. For the past twenty years he'd spent every waking minute dedicated to turning himself from a kid with nothing into a ruthless business-man. For the past several months he'd had to com-pletely strip away that part of himself in order to pour all of his energy into becoming a father.

Meg Kelly simply let him feel like a *man*.

It was energising. It was addictive. It could so easily prove to be his undoing.

Look at her, he said to himself. *The diamonds, the flashy friends, the artless va-va-voom. She revels in the flash and flare of public life. And look at you, hiding in the shadows.*

In allowing this infatuation to continue he was setting himself up to lose too much—he'd certainly lose Meg, and there was every real possibility he might yet lose Ruby. As for the fact that he could look in the mirror and see a guy who'd learnt from the alienation of his past? Gone.

Convinced beyond a shadow of a doubt leaving was the right thing to do, he took one step in that direction when a local reggae band on the other side of the fire struck up their steel drums with a little 'How Deep Is Your Love' Bee Gees action.

His eyes searched for Meg's. She looked up and clapped, radiating pure joy as he'd known she would when he'd put in the request with the enter-tainment director.

Her gaze began flicking back and forth across the

crowd and he knew too that she was looking for him. Instead of sliding deeper into the shadows where he belonged, his feet held firm until her eyes found his.

She smiled with her whole body—ravishing red lips, sparkling blue eyes, the happy shrug of her creamy shoulders. A deeply felt attraction slid through him like slow, hot lava. God, it felt good— like gut instinct, abandon and release. Feelings he'd never allowed himself to come close to feeling for another person his whole adult life.

She made a beeline his way, her friends following in her shimmering wake.

'Zach,' she said on a release of breath when she was close enough he could see the firelight flickering in her eyes.

'Good evening, ladies,' Zach said, purposely including all three. 'Don't you all look beautiful this evening?'

One gave Meg a small shove forward. 'Don't we just.'

Meg glared at her friend, while Zach pretended not to notice.

'Ready for a big night?' he asked.

'I heard rumours of a marshmallow roast,' said the brunette. Tabitha.

'Bring 'em on,' said the blonde, her voice wry.

The hairs on the back of Zach's neck twitched under the blonde's incisive gaze. That one was the journo. At the very least she knew that *something* was happening between her friend and him. She who probably kept a lipstick camera and micro-chip microphone on her person at all times.

Meg slapped her friend on the arm, which he approved of heartily. 'Don't pay any attention to Rylie. She doesn't understand that sweets belong to their own food group the way some of us do.'

When her eyes slid back to him, she let them flick to her friends and with a small shake of her head told him not to worry. He was safe. Ruby was safe.

Then a small smile hooked at the corner of her mouth. *Thanks for the M&M's*, her eyes said.

He blinked back, *My pleasure*.

'Are they actually serving drinks from coconut shells?' Tabitha asked, then she was off.

Rylie, on the other hand, had her hand clamped over Meg's arm as if they'd been soldered together.

Meg blinked at him, her mouth curving in apology. The St Barts crew were a hopeless cover. She knew he was there for her. And while she'd made it perfectly clear to him on more than one occasion that she understood why they should remain miles apart for Ruby's sake, she'd come. The both of them needed their heads read.

'I like the choice in music,' Meg said over her shoulder as Rylie pulled her away. 'Yours?'

'Disco,' he said. 'It's my secret passion.'

She grinned. It lit up the night. And then she was gone.

Zach slid his hands into the pockets of his trousers. He'd put in his promised appearance, meaning he could walk away. Ruby wasn't home so he could slink back to his bungalow and work himself late into the night till his eyes burned and his back ached and he was too exhausted to think about anything but sleep.

He could do that, but instead he decided to stay a little longer. Listen to some Bee Gees. Drink some punch. Eat a marshmallow or two. See where the night took him.

Damn fool.

Meg sat on a straw mat next to Rylie, drinking a mocktail and pretending to watch Tabitha lead a conga line around the fire, but whenever she had half a chance her eyes sought out Zach.

The moment she'd first seen him standing with the fire at his back, feet bare, watching her with the kind of intensity that took her breath away, her skin had warmed as though she'd stepped too near the flames. Even wreathed in hot-pink flowers he was the most wholly masculine creature she'd ever known.

Dark hair slicked back, clean-shaven, and wearing a pale grey linen suit, he *finally* appeared how he should have all along—like the kind of man her father would know by name.

That first moment when she'd been allowed to dream he might be something he was not hadn't been fair. If she'd first seen him looking like this then maybe she would have had her guard up and have avoided this whole mess from the outset.

Who are you kidding? she thought to herself on a slow release of breath. In cargo shorts and a soft faded T-shirt he was beautiful. In a perfectly cut suit he was devastating. A woman would have to be made of far sterner stuff than she to skim past such a creation.

'You having a good time so far?' Rylie asked.

'Mmm?' Meg said, turning to Rylie with the straw of her third pineapple mocktail bitten between her front teeth.

'I feel like we've barely seen you enough to make sure you're actually relaxing as promised.'

Meg raised an eyebrow. 'If you actually turned up to any of the scheduled events rather than leaving me to fend for myself that wouldn't be the case.'

'I'm here now.'

Meg bumped her friend with her shoulder. 'So you are. And I'm glad. This is fun. Especially since Tabitha is so on form, and thankfully not trying to rope us into her insanity.'

'Too true. And, now that I am here, is there anything you'd like to catch me up on? The weather, perhaps? Petrol prices getting you down? Anything happen in the past couple of days you'd like to let off your chest?'

She knew what Rylie was asking. And it was fair enough. They were best friends. Had been since school. Maybe she could give her a little sugar, so long as she gave nothing away about Zach or Ruby. But to do that she'd have to give too much of herself away as well. The myriad reasons why she couldn't just throw herself at him and be done with it went deeper than even Rylie knew.

'The weather, then,' Meg said, tilting her head towards the heavens. 'Look at that sky. Have you ever seen so many stars? Hasn't this been the most beautiful night?'

Rylie paused a long moment before glancing across the fire towards the man they were both pretending not to be talking about. 'Absolutely gorgeous.'

On a sigh Meg said, 'You have no idea.'

A gorgeous man and a gorgeous dad. It was the second part that was making it so easy for her to fall for him, while also making it impossible for her to have him.

She'd never gone through the grieving process the doctors had warned her she might when she'd convinced them to give her the operation that would take away her chance of conceiving a child. All she'd wanted was to do whatever *she* could to stop her father from ever getting the chance to bully another kid again.

She was beginning to fear that was what the faint but now constant ache in her heart was—fissures that had existed in her happy facade since the morning she woke up in Recovery. Only now, as she understood fully for the first time what she'd given up, those fissures were turning into cracks big enough to split her in two.

'Can you do me a favour?' Meg asked.

'Anything. Always.'

'I don't want to be missing any more. In the press, I mean. Dylan texted me today. Apparently the snippet *Chic* ran online a couple of days back has grown legs. I'd rather not be hounded by people with mobile cameras any more than usual this week.'

'I'll get onto my contact at *Chic* and give them the word,' Rylie said. 'Where do you want to be instead of missing?'

Here. 'Anywhere but here.'

'May I ask why?'

Meg tucked her chin against her shoulder and glanced at her friend. 'I wish I could tell you, but it's complicated.'

'Okay, for now. I'm not so silly to think wheat-grass juice is the reason you're glowing like you are. Tell your man he can do as he pleases, I'm looking the other way.'

Meg gave Rylie a quick hug.

Tabitha chose the perfect moment to twist her

way out of the line and head on over, laughing as though she could barely draw breath.

'You are a maniac,' Meg said, her voice still slightly ragged.

Tabitha slumped down onto the straw mat beside them. 'Every party we ever have from now on should be exactly like this.'

'With nobody we know as guests and no alcohol?' Rylie asked.

Tabitha shrugged. 'Why not? I know the wellness class we took the first day was all about finding balance, but sometimes I think you need to let yourself go completely *off* balance too. It's a yin and yang thing.'

Off balance. That was the term Meg had been reaching for to describe how Zach made her feel.

He was intensely private while her life was splashed about the papers so regularly she might as well have been living in her own reality TV programme. He saw family as something to safeguard, not to flaunt. His life was so far removed from her own as to be completely foreign.

This was a man trying so hard to be worthy of his daughter, if he knew how low she'd sunk, how desperate a measure she'd taken in order to pull herself back out into the bright lights, would he understand? Or would he think her ridiculous? Hopeless? Weak? All the things she'd been told she was by the one man who ought to have been her fiercest champion. If even her father couldn't see the good in the real her, what hope did she have with anyone else?

He shifted in the firelight, all shadowy angles and dark good looks.

This man had given her chocolate when she'd needed chocolate. He'd given her disco when she'd needed disco. Would he, *could* he, be the one she could trust to accept her just as she really was?

'As much as it pains me to admit,' Rylie said to Tabitha, 'you may be onto something with this *off balance* thing.'

'I hear that,' Meg whispered.

When the party had well and truly wound down, Zach found Meg standing by the bar alone—a bright red firecracker amongst the few shadowy forms lingering till the end.

'Did you get your fair share of marshmallows?' he asked when he was close enough to breathe in her subtly exotic perfume.

She turned to him with a coconut shell curved into her palm and a straw in her mouth. That mouth. If Zach had ever had cause to believe in heaven and hell that mouth was enough to convince him of both.

'I've eaten far more than my fair share. But it's too late. There's no getting them back now. You had a good night?'

'Tonight hiding in plain sight finally caught up with me. My right hand is bruised from pressing local flesh all evening.'

Her eyes smiled as she sucked on her straw. 'So how was it being Mr Social?'

'One couple had me pinned for half an hour trying to get me to join their pyramid scheme.'

She laughed so hard she tucked her drink to her chest so as not to spill it. 'If you want I can give you some hints on how to extricate yourself quickly and politely so that they leave thinking you were lovely but somehow certain they'd better not go near you again.'

'You are a woman of many hidden capabilities, Ms Kelly.'

She raised one thin eyebrow. 'And then some. Now come on, you must have met some nice people.'

'I did.' Most were surprisingly decent. Warm, welcoming, enthused that he'd seen such value in their beautiful region to create the resort. He said, 'One local businesswoman had some fantastic ideas about marketing local produce around the country using the resort label. I might even look into it while I'm here.'

She grinned. 'I told you schmoozing had its perks.'

'So you did.' He glanced around. 'Where are your chaperones?'

'Rylie needed her beauty sleep and Tabitha practically had to be carried back to the room, she so wore herself out dancing.'

When she smiled at him she made him feel as if he were sixteen again with possibilities he'd never even imagined opening up before him. He felt as if he could take on the world. He felt as if he were standing on unstable ground.

He waved an arm away from the bright bar. Together they walked around the edge of the beach to a place the firelight didn't quite reach.

She slid her bare feet sensually through the sand. Her fingernails and toenails had been repainted blood-red. She smelled of jasmine. Her skin glowed warm and creamy in the firelight. Escaped tendrils of her hair flickered away from her lovely face in the light summer breeze. Heat curled deep within his abdomen.

His voice was rough when he said, 'I've had a question I wanted to ask you all night.'

She clutched her coconut shell to her chest and looked at her feet. 'And what's that?'

'Did you seriously have *that* dress in your suitcase this whole time?'

She laughed. 'A girl never knows when she's going to need a party frock. Besides, the girls packed my bags for me. You'll be shocked to discover coming to a wellness retreat was their idea.' She glanced sideways. 'You look very smart yourself.'

He puffed out his chest. 'I always do.'

'Mmm. But there's just something extra special about you tonight that I can't put my finger on.'

She put her finger on the fullest part of her bottom lip instead. The urge to drag her into the reeds and finish what they'd started the day before, to give in and let instinct and abandon bring release, was almost overwhelming.

Until she asked, 'So did you choose hot pink for your little necklace there?'

Zach glanced down at his shirt only to be reminded of the wilting lei. 'Give me a break—everyone got one coming in.'

'Do you see me wearing one?'

'They must have run out before you got here.'

'Likely excuse.' She slid the straw into her mouth and grinned.

And now you're flirting, he said inside his head. *Of course you're flirting. Just look at her. I mean, really look at her.* He did. She took his breath away.

They hit the far side of the fire and as one took up residence on an empty straw mat. The bonfire no longer blazed, but embers glowed red-hot at the base of the gently licking flames.

'It's very quiet out here all of a sudden,' she said, her voice soft.

'I think we may officially be considered stragglers.'

'Most socially uncool.'

'No need to panic quite yet. We won't be the very last. I'm told there's always one fellow hanging about ready to douse the fire once all's said and done.'

'Then our party reputations will live to see another day!' she said, but he saw in the flicker of her eyes that she heard what he'd really been telling her. They had a chaperone of sorts after all.

She crossed her legs frog style, sitting her drink on her far side and laying her hands in her lap—they fast disappeared into her ample skirt—as she looked into the fire.

Silence stretched between them. He wondered if she could feel the same electricity running up and down her arms that was creating havoc over his.

When she blatantly asked, 'So where's Ruby tonight?' he knew without a doubt that she was well aware.

CHAPTER NINE

THE fact that Meg had to be the one to remind him of the participant in their relationship who wasn't there brought Zach solidly back to earth.

Habit had him slamming his lips shut tight. But then Meg tucked loose strands of hair behind her ear and shot him an encouraging smile. And he couldn't deny, even to himself, that talking to her helped. More than talking to Felicia, or the teachers at Ruby's school, or the social workers who came to the house once a week.

Maybe it was the fact that she would be leaving in a few days. Maybe it was because sometimes she seemed to understand Ruby more than even he did. Or maybe it was because he simply enjoyed talking to her.

For whatever reason, he said, 'She's sleeping over at her friend Clarissa's house. Her first sleepover since moving here. She was so excited when the invitation came through this morning I couldn't say no.'

'Did she tell you about the invitation before or after she made you pancakes?'

He thought back. 'After.'

Meg laughed softly. 'Getting you all nice and buttered up before going in for the kill. I love it.'

The affection in Meg's voice didn't surprise him, but again it moved him. Because of this woman, parts of himself he'd thought long since turned to dry ice had begun to melt. And he wasn't the only one.

He patted the chest of his jacket and felt inside the card Ruby had presented to him that morning. A card she'd made, addressed to Meg. He'd brought it with him with every intention of giving it to her. He even got as far as reaching inside and touching the pink cardboard before his fingers curled into his palm.

Even as he'd slid the card into his jacket earlier that evening, he'd known he couldn't *ever* tell Meg about the card.

Letting Ruby develop a fondness for her was a bad idea. A kid could only have the object of their affection snatched away from them so many times before they learnt it hurt less to simply never form attachments at all. It was his duty to protect Ruby from that kind of hurt as well. As such he could only in good conscience encourage friendships he knew would last.

Meg turned to him with a wide, lovely, genuine smile, and he wished he could be as conscientious with himself. He let his hand slide out of his coat pocket, empty.

She waggled a finger at him and said, 'If I didn't know better I'd think you've read the book after all.'

'Which book is that?'

'*How to Father a Girl*. It's extremely hard to track down and even more difficult to decipher. Lots of hieroglyphics and double talk. But you seem to be following along beautifully.'

'I don't always get that same feeling from Felicia.'

Meg raised an eyebrow. 'Do tell.'

He baulked. Then convinced himself that while keeping Ruby a step removed was one thing, sharing pieces of *his* experiences was fine. In fact, so far it had done him nothing but good. 'She seemed to think I ought to keep Ruby home from Clarissa's because a) she did have a sore throat, or b) she'd been hamming it up. Either way she should be spending the weekend in bed.'

'You overrode the nanny?' Her eyes widened. 'Brave man.'

Zach laughed. 'Letting Ruby have some fun felt right.' He scooped up a handful of sand and let it run slowly through his fingers as he remembered. 'Then after it was settled, for some reason I winked at her. I've never, not once in my entire life, winked. Didn't even know I knew how. And you know what the rascal did?'

'What?'

'She giggled. No more amazing a sound have I heard in my entire life.'

Meg pulled her knees back to her chest and wrapped her arms around them. 'I knew it,' she said on a sigh. 'You've so-o-o read the book.'

Zach brushed the sand from his hand and glanced at her from the corner of his eye. In the semi-darkness the angle of her body was outlined in gold from the dying fire—all curled into itself like a ball of shimmering red fabric. It wouldn't matter who her father was, or the size of her trust fund, she would draw the eyes of those who knew quality when they saw it wherever she went.

He took in a deep breath, wood smoke tickling the back of his throat. 'I may be faking it well enough to fool you, and perhaps even Felicia and Ruby. But the grim truth is I know next to nothing about kids, and less about girls.'

'Many, *many* eons ago little Zach was seven.'

'That is so. Yet my hope is that Zach at seven and Ruby at seven have very different experiences.'

'Why's that?'

The night was so quiet, the fire so mellow, the air so warm, Meg's voice and presence in the darkness so reassuring. The uncomfortable truth of his child-hood balanced on the tip of his tongue for a moment before he swallowed it down. He didn't talk about it. Didn't even like thinking about it. If having stopped flying to the ends of the earth and back meant all that purposely lost baggage might yet catch up with him…

He said, 'She's a girl, for one thing.'

Meg laughed and it echoed through him hollowly. All that virgin trust between them had been built for nought if he could still feign his feelings so easily. But it was too late to tell her now. The moment had passed.

'To tell you the truth,' she said, 'what girls think, what we like, what annoys us, what we want isn't really all that different at Ruby's age or mine.'

'And that is?'

She laughed again. This time he was quick enough to close down the exposed parts of himself so, instead of it making him feel so cool and alone inside, her laughter skittered hot and fast across his skin like sparks from the fire.

Her knees fell towards him, her hand reached out to give her balance and he could see more of her face in the firelight. 'Better I don't say. The more you think you know about womankind, the more you realise you don't know. I'm not being any help to you at all, am I?'

'You are. More than you know.'

'Really?' The flicker of surprise in her voice caught him off guard.

'Really,' he said, infusing the word with as much gravity as he could.

She watched him for a few long, hot moments before finding the fingernails of her right hand unexpectedly intriguing. 'Well, of course I'm helping. I was a seven-year-old girl a lot more recently than you were a seven-year-old boy.'

'That'll be why.'

She smiled. He caught it at the fire-lit edge of her profile. A sexy curve of her mouth, a softening of her wide blue eyes. Heaven help him, he could have kissed her then and there. In front of the lingering fire-douser and anyone else who'd cared to hang about once the food and drinks were gone.

Then she had to go and ask, 'Did you always want kids?' and it was as good as a cold shower.

'Never.' The all too illuminating answer shot from his mouth like some kind of penance for his earlier cowardice. But it was out there now. So he went the only way he knew—forward.

'My lifestyle was not conducive to kids. Or a family of any sort. I was on a plane twice a week. I've lived in hotel suites my whole adult life. The only real-estate I've ever owned was commercial. Any relationships I've had had to fit into that way of life, period.'

'And when you first found out about Ruby?'

'When my lawyer rang with the news I thought it was some kind of cruel joke. But when I hung up the phone it felt as though I'd been waiting for that call all my life.'

'Simple as that, she changed your mind?' she asked, her voice gentle.

'In a heartbeat. It's the strangest thing, but now I can barely remember my life without her.'

The fire crackled as a log split and those above spilt into the gap. Zach came to from far, far away, a whole other lifetime. He glanced across at Meg. Her face tilted to watch the sparks that fluttered up into the darkness. Without the play of expressions that continuously gave her away, he had no idea what she was thinking.

'How about you?' he asked on a whim.

She licked her lips and her brow furrowed for a moment before she turned to him with a breezy smile. 'Kids? Gosh, no. Wherever would I find the time?'

'You're just saying that to make me feel better for admitting I felt that way.'

'Not at all. I promise.' Again he thought he caught a hint of a frown, but it was too dark to really tell. Whatever it was it was soon swallowed by the kind of overbright smile he knew better than to trust. 'Don't get me wrong—my nieces are two of my favourite people in the entire word. I love them to distraction. But it's not on the cards for me.'

'Why?'

He could tell she was really looking at him, and he wished there were some way of turning on a light. Of looking into those bright eyes and knowing what she was thinking before she said it. Being a step behind felt…disquieting somehow.

She eventually said, 'Even apart from the whole

cameras-outside-your-front-door thing, the life of a Kelly kid is not an easy one. The pressure to be the best, the brightest, every day a winner is immense. And that's not changing any day soon.'

'Your nieces are going through this now?'

Again she paused. *Come on*, he thought, *I could do it, so can you.* 'I find myself quietly sabotaging the process wherever I possibly can. I sneak them junk food when their dad's not watching. I teach them swear words in French, which my father doesn't speak. If I babysit I let them wear pyjamas all day. I let them be kids.'

'Talk about maternal instincts,' he said with two raised eyebrows.

She stared at him as if he had grown horns. As if he was missing the point entirely. Then her hand moved to rest on her belly. She scrunched her hand into a fist before looking away and reaching out to grab her toes.

'Instincts or no, unlike you I'm hardly going to have one appear out of the woodwork so that's the end of that.' She shook it off. Literally, her whole body gave one great shiver, before she said, 'Okay. Moving on. Here's something *you* can take to the bank. You ready?'

'Always.'

'Meg's crash course on Raising a Girl 101. Ruby will make friends you don't like, she'll see movies that'll make your eyes pop out of your head, listen to music that makes your ears ache, she'll diet when she doesn't need to, and eat ice cream for breakfast, and she'll meet boys you wish had never been born. Roll with the punches for your own sake. And for hers, let her know no matter what happens she always has a safe place to go home to.'

He nodded, though his head was reeling with points one and two, much less the rest. 'That's why I took on the house here. To give her somewhere near her familiar haunts to come home to.'

'Nu-uh, Mr Jones. By home, I mean *you*. This is the clincher, the one thing you should get tattooed to your arm. No matter what happens, no matter what she does, always, *always*, make sure she knows you love her. That's what will keep her coming home.'

Zach realised he was holding his breath. But he didn't let it go until his lungs began to burn from inaction.

Love. *Love*. Love? The more times he said the word, the less sense it made.

What did he know about love? He'd fed Ruby, clothed her, given her shelter, filled her room with trinkets, let her have her little rebellions as some kind of compensation for not having a mother. But love?

If his own childhood had taught him anything it was that love was a sham. A fickle fairy tale. If loving someone as much as he'd loved some of his foster parents didn't ensure they loved him back, what was the point?

He breathed deep and buried his face in his palms. What a hypocrite. He'd been busy convincing himself he was all about the fatherly care, when all the while he was actually dolling out the same kind of veiled neglect of his childhood without even realising it.

That poor, *poor* kid. Baking him pancakes, picking him wildflowers. At least she was trying to show him she loved him. While he hadn't given her a single clue that he loved her too.

He loved her. Of course he damned well loved her. He'd have been some kind of fool to have changed his life so completely had he not.

He blinked into the fire. Stunned. Apparently never being shown how did not make him as incapable as he'd always believed.

He glanced at Meg. Their gazes tangled a moment longer than could ever be considered merely friendly.

Meg raised her eyebrows. 'Are you okay?'

'Terrified,' he said before he could censor himself.

She laughed softly. Sadly even. 'Then you know you're not perfect. You know you have limitations. That's a good thing. Believe me. What happened to Ruby's mum?'

The last part came so out of the blue it shocked Zach right out of his funk. 'Cancer. It was quick. Ruby didn't even know till it was all over.'

'No! Oh, the poor pet. And Isabel had really never told you about Ruby?'

He shook his head. 'Our relationship had been casual. It ended as easily as it had begun. Still she was very clear in her will that she wanted me to have custody. For that one fact I have to forgive her the rest.'

'Was it really that easy? I know I'm speaking out of turn, but even I don't feel like *I'm* ready to forgive her and I didn't even know the woman.'

She hadn't even had to tell him so. He'd seen the fight in her eyes. Like a lioness protecting her cub. When had this fireside flirtation suddenly become so intense?

He said, 'Over something that important, it was either forgive or let it burn for ever. The choice was simple.'

One dark curl draped over her pale shoulder as she wrapped her arms tight about her knees again. And there they sat, in loaded silence for a good couple of minutes before she finally said: 'My father's sick. You've probably heard.'

He didn't nod. He didn't need to. A person would have to be a hermit, a far more dedicated one than he was, not to know Quinn Kelly had heart problems. 'How's he doing?'

She nodded vigorously. 'Exceptionally well, the old warhorse. So far as I know. He's retired. Plays golf a lot. Eats the kind of food your chef would applaud.'

'That's good news, then.'

She nodded, but it wasn't as effusive. She was a million miles away. 'It gets a girl to thinking.'

'About?'

She scrunched up her nose. 'Things far too blah to go into on such a beautiful night. I'm sorry. Where were we? Ruby.'

Back to Ruby. Always Ruby. It occurred to him then that she might be using his daughter as a shield as much as he had been. He couldn't help but wonder why.

'Meg.'

'Zach,' she said in a mock-sombre voice.

'Tell me.'

She focused on the flowers around his neck. 'It's just all this stuff that I haven't thought about in years that has shuffled up to the surface in the last little while. And then you sit there all noble, making forgiveness sound so easy when I just don't think I could—'

'Tell me,' he said again.

She blinked at him. All big blue eyes and down-turned mouth. 'I can't believe I'm about to…God, where do I begin?'

His voice felt unusually tight as he said, 'Wherever you see fit.'

'Okay,' she said with a hearty sigh. 'There's this one memory that's been playing on my mind. Years ago my father was given an Honorary Doctorate of

Commerce by a university in Melbourne. He'd never gone to uni, never even finished high school, so it was a matter of immense pride. One of my brothers had scraped his knee or something equally boyish, so Mum waited at the hotel to be taken with them in the town car and my father drove himself, with me there, at my mother's insistence, to keep him company. This was years before GPS.'

She looked to him. Her eyes narrowed, almost pleading he get her to stop. He just nodded. *Go on.*

'Anyway, when he finally admitted he was lost he gave me the street directory and told me to show him how to get there. I'd never used one before, couldn't pronounce half the street names, so I read the map wrong and we were late. Less than five minutes, but late is late.'

She stopped again. Licked her lips. Her hands were shaking. The tension streaming off her was palpable. He could feel his pulse beating in his temples.

'What did he do?' Zach asked, half not wanting to know, half needing her to trust him enough to tell him.

'Before the engine had even come to a halt he turned on me. With such venom.' She shook her ponytail off her shoulder to hide the flinch as the memory came at her. 'I was careless, ridiculous, stupid and I had to find my own way back to the hotel to teach me to take heed of where I was and who I was with. By the time I made it to the hotel it was after dark, my mother was beside herself and my father had holed himself up in his room. His doctorate thrown onto the front table of the suite as though it was rubbish.'

Her eyes flickered to his—dark, grave, wounded. Eyes so beautiful they should never be made to look that way. His fingers curled into fists and adrenalin like he'd never felt shot through him.

'How old were you?'

'About Ruby's age. Maybe a little younger.'

He'd known it the moment she'd started telling the story. Hearing her admit as much still made him want to hit something. Or more particularly someone.

'It wasn't the first time,' he said matter-of-factly.

She shrugged and seemed to disappear even further inside her ample skirt. 'Ever since I can remember he'd always been distant. Working a lot. But the first time he took it out on me was the time I told my nanny I was adopted. I thought it was because I'd dare think not being one of them was a more attractive option.'

'And now?'

She let out a long, shaky breath. 'Now I wonder if I had it all backwards. There have always been rumours…' She swallowed, and looked at him, her big, blue eyes begging him to say the things she couldn't.

Zach said, 'You mean his affairs?'

'Not the kind of thing a parent can keep from

their kid when even rumours make the papers.' Her mouth twisted, but a gleam had lit her eyes, as though her strength was returning now she wasn't the only one bearing the load. 'I've often wondered if I was an afterthought. A way to keep their marriage together. If so, it worked. But while my mother never gave a hint of it, the only way I could make sense of my father's behaviour was that I was a reminder of the worst time of his life. That he regretted it. And regretted me.'

'Even if that's true it's not your fault.'

She shrugged. 'I know. I do. And I don't even care any more. At least I thought I didn't. I don't even know why I brought it up.'

Zach understood all too well. 'You've made it very clear exactly why I need to always put Ruby first.'

'I did? I guess I did. And don't you forget it!'

Her soft mouth turned up into the echo of a familiar smile. As they looked into one another's eyes the night stretched and contracted, and once again they communicated more in the silence than mere words could ever say.

Ruby's card began to burn a hole in his top pocket. If ever there was a moment for him to take a risk and give it to her…

And then she yawned. 'And on that note now seems like a good time to escort me back to my room.'

She flapped her hands at him. He pulled himself to his feet before pulling her after him. As they stood face to face her perfumed scent washed over him, delicate and delicious.

All he'd have to do was slide a hand around her neck and pull her to him and that mouth would be all his. The urge to kiss her, to take away the hurt, to give her something warm and wonderful to think about instead was overwhelming.

But she wasn't some gorgeous young thing putting her hand up for a one-night stand. She'd had an intense night. Her thoughts were so obviously still scrambled. He'd be taking complete advantage.

'One last question,' he said, his voice low and rough.

She raised one sexy eyebrow.

'It's about Ruby. I know, I know, I'm getting predictable.'

The corner of her mouth twitched as though she knew exactly what he was doing. 'Shoot.'

'Should I get her a pet? A rabbit maybe?'

She let go of his hands and backed away from the beach towards the resort, towards the end of the night. 'You can't get her a rabbit! They're a pest in Queensland. Start with a goldfish. Let her choose it. Let her name it whatever she wants. She'll be putty in your hands.'

He caught up in three long strides. 'You had a fish?'

'I was a terrible pet owner. I always forgot to feed them, and they had a habit of leaping from the tank in desperation to leave me. But Mum just kept on replacing them. A dozen fish must have died to save the poor woman from having to tell me what was happening.'

'What did you name your first fish?'

She bit back a smile. 'Luke Skywalker. I so-o-o wanted to grow up to be Luke.'

'And now?'

'Now I know better. Han Solo is the bomb.'

CHAPTER TEN

MEG felt more than a little shaky as she walked slowly beside Zach up the white stone path leading away from the lake back to the resort.

What a mess. The things she'd said, the things she'd admitted. So many years she'd kept them deep inside. And then along came Zach and her tightly reined-in emotions were in a tailspin.

There was only one conclusion. She was falling for him. She might as well have been running around with a pair of scissors in her hand. It was only a matter of time before she got seriously hurt.

She had no idea if it was ten at night or three in the morning. The moon told her nothing as she had no sense of direction. The grass was grey and dewy, low cloud cover hovered higher up the path, lending a magical feeling to the place. If she weren't feeling as highly strung as a thoroughbred she might even be able to enjoy it. Instead all she could think about was the man walking silently at her side.

At the very least she knew he'd taken from her shambolic confession what she'd wanted him to—that the foundations of his whole relationship with Ruby were being forged *right now*. The good moments, the pancakes-for-breakfast moments, should be the ones she remembered too.

But even knowing she'd done a selfless thing didn't stop her from feeling like a bowl of jelly on a shaky table.

She slowed her steps before she tripped over her numb feet. Zach's slowed to match.

'Zach?' she said, her voice so croaky she cleared her throat. 'Can I just ask, the things I told you before, I—'

He shook his head and held up a finger an inch from her mouth. Her words dried up in her throat.

Zach's voice was deep when he finally opened his mouth to speak. 'My parents passed away when I was five years old. With no other family I grew up in a slew of foster homes and state-run children's homes—some fair, more atrocious. It didn't matter which, I was still pushed in and pulled out again months later, again and again, with no warning and no word as to why. I had no consistent contact with any one person—no supervisor, no parent, no other foster child—until the day I turned sixteen and I caught a bus to Sydney and began my life.'

Meg realised she was breathing heavily. 'God,

you must think me a schmuck. Complaining about my father when yours wasn't even—'

'No,' he said with a stilling hand on her shoulder. 'Don't do that. No comparing. We each need to own what we've been dealt or we'll never be able to move on.'

She nodded. Then laughed softly to release the pent-up energy coursing through her starting at the point where his strong hand lay upon her bare shoulder. 'You're making me think I ought to have listened harder in wellness class.'

She shook her head, angry at herself for being flippant when talking about anything real. If there was ever a time to not go there, this was it.

She looked up at Zach—tall, dark, divine. 'Have you really owned your past?'

He made a clicking noise with the side of his mouth. 'Please. Why do you think I keep building bigger and better wellness resorts? I'm looking to prove I'm better than my past as much as the next man. But in the past few days I have come to understand a little more about what my foster parents went through. Not taking me in with open arms had little to do with me at all. They would have had to have been masochists to have given that kind of emotional investment to a child they knew would never be theirs. Knowing there's even a minute chance is akin to emotional torture…'

His voice petered off.

'But Ruby—'

'Might still not end up with me.'

'What?' Meg said, her voice like air. 'How?'

'We have up to a year for the state to decide if I am a fit guardian,' Zach said.

Meg's heart squeezed as she remembered the look in Zach's eyes when he'd said his life had changed in a heartbeat when Ruby had come along. The look in Ruby's eyes when she'd proudly said who her father was. 'How long have you had her so far?'

'Seven months, eight days.'

Meg bunched her dress to keep her hands busy lest she do something stupid like hug the guy.

She couldn't even imagine the daily torture it must be to have something so wonderful within reach, knowing it might yet be snatched away. She glanced up at his beautiful profile. Okay, so maybe she could imagine it just the tiniest little bit.

She placed a hand on her heart. 'If there's *anything* I can do. Write a letter of recommendation. Talk to the judge. My family has connections the likes of which you wouldn't believe.'

Before he could be too proud to turn her down, she held out a hand close enough she could feel the warmth of his breath washing against her skin.

'Forget you're not a fan of hoopla. If you need to in order to fight for Ruby, use me for all I'm worth. My notoriety has to be good for something more than invites to every party in town, right?'

He wrapped his fingers around her hand, sliding them through hers until they were intertwined. 'I was going to say thank you.'

'Oh. Well, then, you're welcome.'

She glanced at him, the dark silhouette striding alongside her in the near darkness. Things were even more complicated than she'd imagined. A little girl. A custody battle. And all remarkably hush-hush. How he did it alone, with no family support and with such integrity, she had no idea.

'Is that why you don't do press? You don't like talking about your background?'

'I didn't like being judged for something I had no control over then and I still don't.'

'Why?'

She looked up at him too late to notice how tight his jaw had become.

'If people tell you you're crap often enough, you begin to believe it.'

'You don't think I know that?'

'I say don't give them the chance.'

'I say find a way to negate it so that it can no longer hurt you. There's nothing at all shameful about it. Who you've become is amazing.' She looked down at her toes sticking out of her Grecian sandals. 'I mean, the story of how you got here is amazing. Think about all the foster kids you could help if they knew how you'd pulled yourself up by your own socks to become who you are.'

'Not going to happen. I have to think of Ruby.'

'And what about her?' she asked. 'Are you ever going to tell her where you came from? And if you do will you swear her to silence? Or keep her locked up here for ever to protect yourself from the sting of other people's opinions?'

'What about your father?' he shot back.

'What about him?'

He pulled her closer, until they came to a stop. 'He's a bully. Hell, Meg, he was emotionally abusive to you. Yet of all the parts of your life on show, why has that never come out? Why not show other young girls that their own expectations of themselves are the ones that matter, not what other people think they should be?'

She tried to expertly extricate her hand from his, a move she'd pulled a thousand times, but it was as though he had been waiting for it.

He took her other hand so she was stuck facing him when he said, 'Forget Ruby for a moment— what about all the other little girls who read magazines and look up to you as a role model?'

That was what her volunteer work was for! So what if the girls whose hair she braided and the boys she played cops and robbers with didn't know who the woman behind the bleached-blonde wig and brown contacts was? At least she was there.

She itched to tell him so. To say out loud that working at the Valley Shelter was the most rewarding thing she'd ever done and that every moment she spent flirting with a camera lens so that her rotten bloody father got the chance to muck about with someone else's hard-earned savings felt more and more like hard work.

Especially when even having looked death in the eye it hadn't once occurred to him to make retribution.

But the old fear of being thought ridiculous for thinking herself more valuable than she was rose up her ankles, her calves, her waist, until it reached her throat and she sputtered like an old car whose engine would never again come to life.

'I do think of them,' she said. 'I am doing what I can. In my way. Just not the way you mean.'

He closed his eyes a moment and took a calming breath. He was probably counting to ten. Her brothers did that all the time.

When he opened his eyes they were deliberately calm. As such she wasn't nearly prepared for his next words.

He said, 'So you're not simply filling the void of not being loved by your father with being loved by the entire world?'

She coughed out an incredulous laugh, and dragged her hands from his to slam them onto her hips. 'Are *you* trying to tell *me* that giving up your life for Ruby isn't your way of making *someone* in the world love you back?'

Silence stretched between them as taut and dangerous as an overstretched rubber band.

Until Zach said, 'Maybe you're right. Maybe that's how this all began. But I do love her. And as soon as she comes home from Clarissa's, I'll tell her so because it's important for a little girl to know her dad loves her. Or so someone I trust told me.'

Meg shook her head. This was backfiring big time. If he pulled when she pushed she was never going to be rid of him. Instead, he was being gorgeous and warm and understanding and a tower of strength and a wonderful dad.

With a growl at the moon she headed back up the path again.

'Meg,' he said from behind her.

She waved a go-away hand at him.

He jogged to catch up to her, this time spinning her to face him with the gentlest of pressure at her elbow.

'Thanks ever so much for being such an enchanting escort, but I'm sure I can make it back from here.' She glanced at her surroundings to discover they had gone a ways past the Waratah House turn-off and had found themselves outside one of the lovely little bungalows on the way to Zach's place. A light was on over the porch.

'I could do with a coffee right about now—how about you?' he asked.

She whirled to stare at him. The moon was now almost completely obscured by cloud and his eyes were nothing more than patches of black within his shadowed face. 'Now what are you talking about?'

He waved a hand towards the bungalow. 'I use it as my office. Some nights I stay over rather than heading back to the house. So the pantry is well stocked with all sorts of delights, including coffee.'

'Oh,' she said, his meaning not even the slightest bit obscured by the fact that she couldn't see his eyes. He'd been leading her here the whole time. To his cosy, empty, private abode. Which had a bed. And coffee.

She licked her lips as her mind whirled a million miles a minute. 'And you kept this from me the whole time? The coffee part, I mean.'

His mouth lifted so the preposterously sexy arc in his right cheek put in a surprise appearance. 'I wasn't prepared to share my coffee with you then.'

'And now?'

He lifted a hand to slide it into the hair at the base of her neck, the tug of his warm fingers almost too much to bear.

'I'd say things have changed rather dramatically over the past few days. My eyes have been opened in more ways than one. And I only have you to thank. Coffee seems a meagre place to start.'

Meg swallowed, her mouth dry, her blood thundering in her ears until she felt the slightest bit dizzy. There were reasons, good reasons why this couldn't happen, only she couldn't remember one.

He slid his spare hand into his trouser pockets. She imagined she could hear the soft tinkle of keys somewhere on his person.

'Zach—' she said, her voice half appeal, half groan.

'Enough talk,' he said.

He leaned down and kissed her. And she was on her toes, reaching up to him even before he gathered her into his arms.

The raging heat of his kiss swept her away, spiralling her into the cosmos until she could no longer feel her feet. Could no longer remember her name.

Or why they hadn't been doing this all along.

Meg lay on Zach's bed, white cotton sheets tangled about her, his long limbs trapping her in his warm embrace.

She glanced at the clock on the wall. It was only a couple of hours before sunset. Rylie and Tabitha would soon notice her gone. They'd assume where she was, and they'd be right. They'd known she'd end up here before she did. As apparently did Zach. It seemed everyone knew her better than she knew herself.

She tilted her head to watch Zach's sleeping face. The creases at the edges of his eyes had disappeared. His tanned skin looked radiant against the white pillow. A faint line curved down his right cheek, a reminder of the arc that grooved deep when he laughed. He was sleeping like a man with no worries on his mind.

She reached up and slid a curl from his forehead. He didn't stir.

Such gentle strength. She felt it infusing her more with every second she spent in his arms until she couldn't imagine when in her life she would ever have felt this kind of peace, this slowly budding confidence that if she looked deep inside herself she might not be afraid of what she saw.

The words spilled from her lips to his sleeping form before she even knew they were coming. 'I volunteer at the Valley Women's Shelter at least once a week. It's a halfway house for women who've managed to break free of abusive relation-ships but have nowhere else to go. Most have kids. Most have nothing with which to go it alone bar the clothes on their backs. Many are so battered and bruised they can barely talk.'

He shifted and she held her breath. He slid his leg along hers, wrapping his arm tighter about her, sending warm waves of pleasure all over her body. But his eyes remained closed. She waited until the sensations rolling across her skin dissipated, and his breaths were once again even and deep.

'I wear a blonde wig,' she whispered, 'contacts, the kind of make-up you'd see in a bad eighties movie, clothes I picked up in a bargain bin at a thrift store. I can walk through a throng of paparazzi in front of my building and they don't turn an eye. The guys at the shelter know me as Daisy. They've never asked questions, just appreciated someone giving their time to play with the kids while the mums have medicals, or to just sit and hold a woman's hand while they tell their stories to the counsellors.'

She took a deep breath and let it out on a wobble.

'Compared with the level of abuse they've been subjected to my dad constantly finding new weird and wonderful ways of letting me know he didn't consider me worthy of the name Kelly was a walk in the park. But I still see myself reflected in their eyes when they talk about how hard it was to finally say "enough". I give cups of tea, and a shoulder to cry on and secretly stashed envelopes full of money to help them start a new life. It's the most worthwhile thing I've ever done and my name has nothing to do with it.'

She let her gaze amble over Zach's beautiful nose, his strong jaw, the smattering of dark hair curling over his chest.

'So there you have it. That's what I do to really make a difference. I just don't shout it out to the world. Not because I'm not proud, or I don't realise it's vitally important. But because it's hard, and it's private, and I do it for myself and for them, not for him and not for the cameras.'

'Thank you,' Zach said, and had it not been for the knot of sheets and his heavy limbs keeping her in bed Meg might well have leapt a foot in the air.

She placed a hand over her thundering heart. 'How long have you been awake?'

'Longer than you have.'

She lay back and blinked up at the ceiling. 'So, just now, you heard everything.'

'Everything.' He snuggled in closer and kissed her on the cheek, right at the edge of her mouth. 'And thank you for telling me.'

She turned to face him. His dark eyes burned into hers. She needn't have searched so desperately for what he was thinking—it was written all over his beautiful face. He did not think her ridiculous. He did not think her a mere party girl. He thought her pretty amazing.

'Thank you for listening,' she whispered before leaning in and placing her lips against his.

And they made love again. Slowly, gently, not once taking their eyes off one another.

A while later Meg fell asleep, knowing without a single doubt that she loved him. Knowing she was never again going to meet someone who saw her, really saw her, as he did. Who made her wonder if the day might yet come when she'd be brave enough to let the rest of the world nearer than skin deep too.

She fell asleep knowing Zach cared for her. Knowing he respected her. Knowing he'd made *love* to her.

She fell asleep knowing that, despite all that,

Zach Jones and his gorgeous blooming little family only reminded her with stark, heart-wrenching clarity what she could never have.

As the sun rose through the bay windows of the bungalow, Zach stood in the bedroom doorway in last night's trousers watching Meg dress.

She stood by his rumpled bed, tying the bow on her dress, the muscles of her back working sexily, a small frown pinched between her brows, and her top teeth biting down on her bottom lip. He couldn't believe there was ever a moment when he'd assumed the Meg Kelly the country adored was all an act. In that moment she was so very, very real.

The diamonds, the flashy friends, the *va-va-voom*, they were the trappings of her life, but not why she was beloved. It came down to the fact that she was a warm, dynamic woman who bled like everyone else, and spent her life making sure those around her didn't hurt as much when they bled too. Whether it was a woman running from an abusive husband, her complicated family, his young daughter, a complete stranger who accosted her, camera in hand, while she vacationed, she had time, she had a smile, she had a way of making them feel better off for having met her.

His hands literally ached with the desire to haul her back into his arms and soak up every bit of vitality she could spare. But he needed to get home.

To be there when Ruby returned. He had things to do. Things to say.

He pushed away from the door and slid his hand down her back, tugging at her dress until he could feel and see the trail of wild daisies tattooed across her lower back.

At his touch her head fell back in pleasure, her hair spilling over her bare skin.

'So what's the story here?' he asked, his fingers tracing the daisy vine, his breath tickling her ear.

She shivered. 'I got it when I was fifteen. Daisies were my favourite flower. Luckily they still are.'

'What? Fifteen? You need parental permission, right? Until you're eighteen?' *Please, God*, he thought, *let that be true*.

She smiled over her shoulder at him. 'Of course you do. Unless your father said no way in hell was his daughter getting a tattoo and you were me. Then you find a way to get whatever you want.'

Her skin was warm and soft until the tattoo made it feel ever so slightly rough. 'Did it hurt?'

'Like hot needles into the bone for two straight hours. Yuh-huh.'

'You really were a tearaway.'

'I could tell you stories.'

He placed a kiss where her neck met her shoulder. 'So tell me.'

She moved so that her hair fell over the spot he'd just been kissing. 'Another time perhaps.'

He pulled back. A sudden chill had come from her direction. He shook it off. Mornings after were always at least some level of awkward. She'd be all right with some space to process it all.

He searched for his shirt from the night before to find it crumpled on the floor. 'Give me a minute to find a T-shirt and I'll walk you back.'

She plonked onto the corner of his bed as she tied the straps of her shoes around and around her calves. 'Best not. The forest has eyes and ears.'

It struck him she'd once again gone there, to Ruby, so fast, and before he had. But then again there was so much about this whole night that had surprised him. Including the fact that eyes and ears no longer seemed such a threat as they had twenty-four hours earlier.

She had been right in accusing him of locking Ruby away to save himself from having to face the demons of his past. And while he didn't want to see Ruby hurt, ever, surely he didn't want her living the kind of emotionally and physically isolated existence he'd lived all the years before she brought him back into the light.

Meg stood, smoothed down her dress, slicked her hair back into a fresh ponytail and looked around to make sure she hadn't left anything behind.

'Come over for morning tea,' he said before he could stop himself.

Meg glanced up at him in obvious shock. She licked her lips before saying, 'And what, skip DIY Colonic Irrigation class?'

He laughed, but he was not to be deterred. 'Let's say around eleven.'

She watched him a few long moments. Her back was to the sun, so he couldn't make out the expression in her eyes. For the first time in hours a familiar hollowness began to expand inside him. He didn't know what to make of it, he only knew he didn't like it.

'Why?'

Good question. 'I promised you coffee last night and we never quite got there.'

'You didn't promise me anything, Zach,' she said, her voice gentle.

'Come over. Drink coffee. The rest we can make up as we go along.'

Another few protracted moments passed in which she just looked at him. Though it felt more as if she was looking through him, her mind a million miles away. 'Should I bring anything?'

The hollowness went away. 'Just yourself.'

She ran her hands down her dress again. 'Okay.'

'We'll see you then.'

She caught the 'we' loud and clear. He could see it in her sudden stillness. In the duration of her indecipherable stare.

'Just you,' he said. 'Not your family. Not your

father. In the privacy of my home. I'm asking *you* to break bread with my daughter and me under comparatively conventional circumstances.'

She nodded. Then said, 'Fine. Till then.'

She leaned into him, her hand pressing against his bare chest as she placed a goodbye kiss on his cheek. He could smell the scent of the lei he'd worn the night before on her skin.

She moved back just far enough to look into his eyes for one dark, hot moment before she walked away.

CHAPTER ELEVEN

LATER that same morning Meg stood in the opening in the stone wall at the edge of Zach's backyard, her fingers gripped tight around a bunch of wildflowers she'd picked along the way.

'What are you doing here?' she asked herself out loud.

She couldn't answer that any more than she could figure out what Zach saw as the end play to all this. She'd made it clear kids weren't part of her life plan and that she wouldn't be the right kind of influence over his. Last night she'd let him off the hook in showing she understood why he would choose Ruby's privacy over any manner of relationship with her.

Last night…

She sighed. It ought to have been their swansong, and a beautiful swansong at that. If only he hadn't had some crazy idea she couldn't fathom. And if only she hadn't gone and fallen in love with the guy.

Her mobile phone buzzed in her pocket, scaring

the bejeezers out of her, and fraying her very last nerves.

She ignored it as she had the last ten times it had buzzed that morning. The moment she'd got back to her room her family—who had mostly left her alone for less than half her allotted vacation time—had decided to rear their relentless heads en masse.

Dylan's voice message had appeared first, taking the edge off her long, luxurious, hot shower: 'Hey, kiddo. Tabby told me where she's taken you. Classic! By now you must be itching for something to take your mind off the boredom. Find a computer, RSVP yourself to the Shyler Benefit in KInG's name for the day you get back.'

No *goodbye*. No *if you happen to be free*. Just do it. She justly ignored him.

During breakfast Cameron's first text message came through: 'U have Dad's *The Iliad*? Urgent… ish. Rosie'd love to read it. What Rosie wants Rosie gets!'

From her newly mobiled-up mother: 'Love you. Miss you.' From her father? Not a whisper. All that water under the bridge and it still wounded.

Angry with herself for letting her father get to her by omission, when Brendan's number blinked on the screen five minutes later she ignored it. Voicemail gave her: 'Mum has a thing next Saturday night. The nanny's night off. You need to look after the girls. Confirm with my secretary ASAP.'

Dylan must have called again as his next message came through straight after: 'How do you feel about co-hosting the Queensland Fashion Awards? You love the idea. I knew you would. Call me ten minutes ago and I'll set you up with press to confirm.'

She'd somehow almost forgotten that this was what her life was like back home—non-stop motion, never saying no, doing everything to be appear cheerful and be inordinately useful. Everybody's favourite girl. She felt exhausted and underwhelmed just thinking about it.

Of course the fact she'd had less than two hours of uninterrupted sleep amidst one of the most stunning, tender, unsparing, magical, revealing nights of her life would likely have made aliens landing on her doorstep an underwhelming experience.

She looked through the brush to the hint of a house beyond. To Zach. She breathed in deep through her mouth and out through her nose, her heart racing as if she'd run five kilometres that morning rather than tucking herself up under the bed covers and hiding the moment she'd snuck back to her room.

As she walked through the backyard a flock of pink and grey galahs settled in a nearby tree. Discarded by Ruby's swing were her skipping rope and a pink bike with a white cane basket and streamers on the handle bars. Had it really only been days since she'd been there before? It felt as if weeks had passed.

The thing that ought to have her walking away kept her moving forward: the chance to see them together. To see if he was as natural a father as she'd trusted. To see if Ruby was as doting a kid as she'd suspected. It would be akin to self-flagellation, but she had to know. To see if that kind of relationship really could exist.

Her phone buzzed again. She whipped it out of her pocket, switched it off and shoved it out of sight.

She headed up the rope bridge that led to the largest structure amongst the string of thatched-roof rooms.

A grey-haired woman came out onto the verandah, and she jumped in fright at seeing Meg bundling her way. 'Aren't you just as quiet as a church mouse?'

I'm as nervous as one, Meg thought. But she conjured up her second-nature Meg Kelly smile, designed to put others at ease, and said, 'I'm Meg. I'm expected.'

The woman's cheeks pinked. She even gave a small curtsy. 'Of course you are, dear. I'm Felicia, Ruby's nanny. You may as well make yourself comfy out here. Zach won't be long.'

Meg handed the motley bunch of flowers over to Felicia, whose eyes widened a tad before a smile snuck into her already copiously creased cheeks.

'How charming. I'll put these in water, shall I?' Felicia then turned and headed along the balcony and across yet another bridge and out of sight.

Feeling like a flibbertigibbet, Meg tugged at her floral peasant top making sure it remained demure, and smoothed down her tight, cropped jeans.

Footsteps came from behind her. She spun around and had to cling to the railing for support against the rush of heat that swept over her as Zach walked down the hall inside the house towards her.

His feet were bare below faded jeans that fitted snugly to his long legs as though he'd owned them all his life. A just as faded coffee-brown T-shirt made the most of his bronzed skin and his dark hair was still wet, as though he'd had a recent shower.

Her heart felt so full it didn't know what to do with itself. Beat? Go bust? Leap from her chest and into his arms?

As Zach hit the sunlight angling into the house she saw Ruby was hiding behind his legs. How alike they looked. Long, lean, dark good looks, fierce intelligence swimming behind their guarded eyes. But it was their natural connection that hit hardest. If he took one short step she would have banged into him, but somehow their rhythm stayed in sync. It was mesmerising. And unbearable.

'You came,' Zach said when he spotted her.

She shrugged, feigning nonchalance she was nowhere near feeling. 'I had nowhere better to be.'

He laughed. 'I won't be putting *that* on the brochures, I can assure you.'

'Smart move.'

They smiled at one another awhile and Meg took solace in the fact that she wasn't the only one who was nervous.

'Now, Ruby,' Zach said, gently uncurling his daughter from behind him, pulling her around in front but keeping two hands on her shoulders. 'You remember Meg, right?'

Ruby's dark eyes stared back at her, testing, deciding whether it served her to admit as much. Meg's heart performed the greatest twitch of its life. Zach had his hands full more than he even realised.

She leaned down to Ruby and murmured out of the corner of her mouth, 'You didn't happen to save me any muffins from the other day, did you?'

Ruby shook her head.

'Mmm.' Meg held a finger to her mouth. 'I'm guessing that's because your dad ate the lot.'

Ruby glanced up at him with wide eyes.

'Men,' she said, rolling her eyes. 'Promise me you'll never make the mistake of thinking they're at all complicated.'

'I won't,' were Ruby's first words. Bright kid.

'On that note,' Zach said, his voice a rumble that skittered along Meg's arms, 'I'll be back in a minute with real food. No muffins. Behave. Both of you.'

Meg smiled back.

He gave her one last, white-hot look before heading inside, jerking her poor heart around all the more. How could he expect her to behave after that?

She sauntered over to a large square outdoor table sitting neatly in the shade of a massive cream, linen umbrella and perched her backside on the edge of a wooden bench seat.

'So, Miss Ruby,' she said, curling a finger at the girl, 'what's the plan for this morning?'

Ruby moseyed near and picked at a knot of wood in another chair. 'Since Dad got to choose who was invited over, I got to pick what we'd eat.'

'Fair enough. So what are we eating?'

Ruby eyed Meg down with wisdom beyond her years. 'I picked peanut butter on white bread. Dad thought you might like something else. I told him you'd like peanut butter on white bread.'

'Well,' Meg said, trying to keep her cool while the kid wrapped herself tighter and tighter around her heart. 'Would you believe that of all the food in all the world, peanut butter on white bread is exactly what I want?'

'I knew it. I liked your pink dress, so it made sense that if I liked peanut butter you would too. Ooh, wait there!' Ruby said, before tearing off inside.

'I'm not going anywhere,' Meg said to the empty doorway, her heart pressing towards the space where Ruby had been.

She shoved her face into her hands. She should never have come. She knew it would only make her love him more. Make her feel for his sweet kid. Make her wonder how she was ever going to go back to a life of smiling and pouting and pretending it was the greatest job on earth.

Unless this didn't have to end. Unless Zach had brought her here with completely non-altruistic intentions. Unless last night had meant exactly as much to him as it had done to her.

Ruby came running out of the house with something behind her back.

Meg sat up and physically wiped the hope from her face. 'What have you got there?'

'I asked Dad to give this to you yesterday but I found it on the hall table this morning. He must have forgotten,' Ruby said, sneaking up onto the bench beside Meg.

As Meg would have done with her nieces, instinct had her putting her arm around Ruby as she opened the gift. Pink cardboard was covered in scraps of cellophane, wrapping paper, leftover art-supply stuff. And inside Ruby had drawn a picture of a woman who could only be her. Brown curly hair. A pink dress. And a pile of chocolate muffins at her feet.

To Meg, it said in rainbow-coloured letters. *Love Ruby.*

Her breath got stuck in her throat. A gorgeous card that Ruby had made for her. A whole day earlier.

Zach hadn't forgotten to give it to her. He was so smitten with this kid there was no way. He was on a high from the smallest of advances they were making. He might even have believed he had her advice to thank for many of them. But deep down he had no intention of either he or his little girl getting too attached to her.

She breathed in and out and somehow managed to talk Ruby through all the delightful nuances of the present knowing Zach had never wanted her to have it.

It had been the smart move. The right decision. That still didn't stop her heart from shrinking until it felt three sizes too small.

'Are you both still in one piece?' Zach asked as he rejoined them.

Meg slipped the card beneath her backside, looked to Ruby, held a finger to her lips, and said, 'Shh.'

Thankfully, Ruby just giggled.

Zach's smiling eyes were full of questions. Of devotion to his little girl. Of so much promise to be the most complete man she'd ever known. Only Meg knew that the promise would never be hers to see fulfilled.

All this and morning tea had only just begun. If she was ever going to get through this she'd have to give the greatest performance of her life.

Zach placed the tray of drinks and a platter of fat fruit and gleaming cheeses and exotic crackers on the table. Her motley bunch of flowers had pride of place in a skinny glass vase in the centre of the tray.

Ruby snuck up onto her knees and pulled out a waxy white flower from the bunch, tore off the stem, and tucked it behind her ear. She did the same for Meg. Then a third for Zach, who leaned down and let her do it.

'They're Ruby's favourite,' he said, running a hand over his daughter's hair.

Meg could have cried.

'Wait here,' Ruby said. 'I have more to show you.' She took off back into the house.

Zach grabbed some loose grapes and threw them into his mouth. He looked at her as if he knew some great secret, when she was the one sitting on the greatest of them all.

'You look ridiculous,' Meg said, staring at the flower. Anywhere rather than in Zach's warm eyes.

He grinned. 'So what were you two up to when I came out here?'

Meg's eyes connected with his and got stuck in all that deep, dark, beautiful, chocolate-brown. 'I have no idea what you're talking about.'

He stared into her eyes. 'You're a terrible liar.'

She blinked, desperately hoping he wasn't as clever as he thought he was. She looked away, and took a couple of strawberries from the platter. 'Ruby seems really happy.'

'I think she just might be. In fact, I think we both

are. At the very least we're both now on the right path to get there.'

Zach leaned forward in his chair. His hands slid across the table until they were almost touching hers. She tried to keep her breaths steady.

'When you get home,' he said, 'you should talk to your father.'

She curled her fingers into her palms. 'About?'

'Meg,' he said, looking deep into her eyes, his voice ever so slightly ragged. 'This is me you're talking to.'

She swallowed. She knew exactly whom she was talking to—the man who'd won her heart. She uncurled her fingers from her palms, slid her hand along the table toward his—

Footsteps sounded on the wooden balcony. They both looked up to find Felicia holding a landline phone. 'Sorry to interrupt, but it's Reception for Meg.'

Meg cursed Reception with every fibre of her being for their terrible timing. Then she realised she hadn't told anyone where she'd be. As if that would stop the Kellys. If this was Dylan trying to pin her down to a dozen PR jobs for the first dozen hours after her return she'd throttle him.

She took the phone, her tone cool as she said, 'This is Meg.'

'Oh, thank God.'

'Rylie?'

'Honey, you have to come back. Now.'

'What's happened?'

'It's Quinn.'

Meg's eyes slammed shut as wave after wave of anger rolled through her. Of all the moments the man could have picked to— The words clogged in her head and anger turned to guilt, which turned to too many emotions for her to keep up.

'Tell me straight,' she said, her voice astonishingly even. 'Is he—?'

'He's had another heart attack.'

'But he's alive,' she said.

'He is. Brendan called my mobile when he couldn't get through to yours. Tabby's packing your stuff and we can be at your car in fifteen minutes.'

'I'll be there.'

She pulled the phone from her ear and suddenly didn't know what to do with it.

Zach was already beside her, sliding it from her shaky grasp. Then his warm arms were around her, pulling her close, wrapping her tight.

'What do you need me to do?' he asked, her ear against his chest feeling the rumble of his words.

I want you to love me. I need you to let me go.

She said, 'I have to go home.'

Home. Her life. Her father. God, could this be it? She realised she had begun to tremble.

Zach, on the other hand, was in complete control. He had already eased her down the bridge and across the yard before she even knew her feet were moving.

'But Ruby,' she said.

'Felicia's looking after her. I'll explain later that you had an emergency and had to go early.'

'What about her peanut butter on white bread? She was so excited.'

His arm at her back slid around her waist until he was cradling her and pressing her forward at the same time. She let him. Let herself steal as much of his kind of strength as she could get while she had the chance.

'Felicia's a pushover,' Zach said. 'Ruby probably has that all the time and they simply don't tell me. Feminine mystery. I'm learning to live with it.' His voice grew deep and close as his lips settled on her hair. 'Now stop worrying about us, and just walk.'

When she tripped over her own feet for the third time, Zach picked her up and carried her. She wrapped her arms about his neck and snuggled in. If he didn't care who saw them like that, then neither did she. It cushioned the several kinds of dread inside her as nothing else could.

He put her down when they reached the garage behind Waratah House. Her momentum propelled her to Rylie, who gathered her up and swept her into the tight back seat of the already packed Jag.

'Take care of her,' she thought she heard Zach's deep voice rumble as the engine gunned.

Rylie said, 'Never fear, Mr Jones. We always do.'

The car backed out of its spot, and Meg looked up to find Zach was a silhouette already too far away for her to see his eyes. Already too far away to thank him. To tell him…anything.

Tabitha drove them out of the high white gates, while Rylie held her hand in the back seat.

It must have been a good deal over an hour later, though it only felt like minutes, when they rounded the final bend of the Pacific Motorway to see the towering silhouette of Brisbane's glass and chrome skyline.

Kelly Tower—the home of the Kelly Investment Group—stood out tall and majestic, a gleaming reminder that she was nearly home. That within minutes she'd be slung back into the frantic, high-pressure, achievement-driven life her whole family led. That once again her father—a man who likely would have preferred it if she weren't even there—was about to become the centre of her life.

If it weren't for the wilting white waxflower she cupped gently in her hand, she might have thought the past few days were all a dream.

CHAPTER TWELVE

A WEEK had gone by when Zach drove up to the imposing wrought-iron gates of the Kelly family's Ascot home.

A week with no clue as to what was happening in Meg's life bar what he read in every newspaper he could get his hands on, hoping he could trust what they said. A week spent living with the memory of her warm body wrapped around his as he slept in his now lonely bed. A week spent remembering that even while dealing with her worst nightmare Meg had still worried that Ruby might be upset about missing out on her peanut butter on white bread.

The gates of Kelly Manor opened as a florist's van trundled down the long, imposing driveway. Mounds of press lurked outside, but none of them pushed into the grounds, showing a measure of respect that surprised him.

He stared them down as they peered into his car

from a relatively safe distance. Him with his little girl in the back seat. His palms sweated so much he had to wipe them on his trousers.

He'd just have to get over it. The few months he was assured of having her all to himself he was no longer going to spend locking her away like some modern-day Rapunzel. The best thing he could do for her was to make sure she felt safe and loved, but also as if her future was one filled with boundless possibilities.

And while his little girl was blooming under his new philosophy, inside that huge house there was another woman in his life who was suffering. And he had no intention of abandoning either one.

He fixed the rearview mirror so he could catch Ruby's eye. 'Honey.'

'Yeah, Dad.'

'See all those people there? They're newspaper and TV reporters. They have cameras, and will get very close to the car. If you don't want your photo taken you can stick your head between your knees.'

'I don't mind.'

He turned to look over his shoulder. To look at his little girl. For a kid who had every reason to be as skittish as a newborn colt, she was one of the most gung-ho people he'd ever met. He could only hope that had a tiny bit to do with him.

'Okay, then,' he said, winking at her, 'here we go.'

He gunned the engine, turned into the driveway. Flash bulbs blinded him enough he had to drive with one hand over his eyes, but he made it through the gate and up the long curving drive in one piece.

'You all right, hon?' he asked Ruby once they were clear of the throng.

She nodded, her eyes wide, before she turned to peek through the tinted back window. 'Why did they want a photo of me?'

He smiled. 'Because you're just so adorable.'

She patted at the pink band around her head that Felicia had shown him how to slide into place in order to keep her long hair from her face. 'Can we ask them for a copy of the picture so I can take it to school? Clarissa won't believe me if I just tell her.'

Zach's smile turned to laughter. 'I'll see what I can do.'

Tracking down a paparazzo for a favour was one of the crazier things he'd ever agreed to. Though when compared with the fortnight he'd had, maybe not.

He pulled his car in behind the red Jag that had taken Meg from him all those mornings ago. His hands gripped tight to the steering wheel as he remembered the haunted look in her eyes as she'd been driven away. He should have come sooner.

He was here now. He hoped that would be enough.

He held Ruby's hand as they walked up the steps towards the Georgian-style manor, passing two life-sized statues of Irish wolfhounds. He tilted his head at the dogs and poked a face. Ruby giggled. And he knew that he wasn't only here for himself—he was here for her.

Within seconds of his using the old-fashioned brass knocker, Meg's mother, Mary Kelly herself, opened the door. He saw Meg in her eyes, the shape of her chin, and the same inability to hide her true feelings from him behind her practised smile.

She was exhausted, she was anxious, but her husband was still very much alive.

Zach said, 'I'm so sorry to intrude, Mrs Kelly. My name is Zach Jones. I own the Juniper Falls Rainforest Retreat and was with Meg when she heard the news about your husband. I was hoping I might be able to check how she and your husband were faring.'

'Of course, Zach, please come right in,' Mary said, welcoming him, a veritable stranger, into her home. This time he saw Meg in her natural warmth.

Ruby tucked in tight behind him so close she might as well have been sewn to his trousers. When Mary saw her, a spark lit her tired eyes. It was Meg all over again. He looked past her, wondering how close Meg might yet be.

Mary bent from the waist, placing her hands on her knees. 'And who might this gorgeous creature be?'

'This is Ruby,' he said. 'My daughter.'

Mary held out a hand and said, 'I'm very pleased to meet you, Ruby. As will my granddaughters be. Violet and Olivia are playing outside in the rear gardens now with their uncle Dylan. Would you like to come and say hello?'

Zach glanced past Mary again and wondered if everyone was playing outside with Uncle Dylan. Then he crouched down to her level and held her hands. 'Would you like to go outside and play? It's entirely up to you.'

Mary held out a hand. Ruby took it. Trusting. Sociable. Like her mother.

'James,' Mary said to a liveried man Zach hadn't even noticed standing by the entrance to what looked like a large sitting room, 'would you kindly take Mr Jones to Meg. I believe she's in the upstairs media room.'

'This way, sir,' James said before heading up the wide, carpeted stairs.

Family photographs lined the staircase wall. Dozens, dating back generations. He'd never had any photographs of his parents, and kept none of his childhood now. The Kelly wall of fame was thoroughly intimidating.

The closer they got to the top of the stairs, the more familiar faces became. Quinn and Mary sailing with two young boys scampering at their feet. The three boisterous-looking brothers, late teens, playing cricket in the backyard. And Meg at the beach, younger than Ruby was now, her bottom lip sticking out while her double scoop of ice cream melted on the ground at her feet.

And look at her now, he thought, his eyes resting on a much more recent picture of her walking down a city street, gorgeous in a silver party dress, pale pink high heels, hair flying as she grinned back at the camera. There was a measure of confidence in her eyes, secret confidence. He alone knew the hard work she'd done to feel as if she'd earned the right to hold her head high.

He reached out to wipe a smudge of dust from the picture.

'Sir, this way,' James said from the top of the stairs, his face discreetly averted.

Zach shoved his hands into his suit pockets and jogged the last few steps.

'Miss Meg is in the room at the end of the hall,' James said. 'Shall I announce you?'

Zach shook his head, gave James a slap on the arm, then headed towards the slightly ajar double doors. He pressed one open. It made no sound.

The large room was filled with overstuffed chairs in old-fashioned plaids and florals, which mixed incongruously with the discreet silver surround-sound speakers, the wall-to-wall built-in book-shelves stacked with DVDs, and the state-of-the-art cinema set-up.

And at the edge of the room, curled up on a tub

chair, staring absently out of the open double windows leading to a small balcony, sat Meg.

His chest clenched at the sight of her in loose jeans, red winter socks and a long-sleeved cream-and-red T-shirt that clung to her curves. She wore not a lick of make-up and her hair had been scragged back into a low bun from which several long curls had escaped. She played absently with her lower lip while some movie he recognised as having not even been released at the cinema played out quietly on the massive projector screen behind her.

Now he was there he realised it was testimony of his years of obstinate will power that he'd managed to go without sight of her for a full week. And now he was there, now she was so close, he couldn't wait a second more.

He planted his feet and cleared his throat.

She glanced up. Dark circles ringed her deep blue eyes, making them look bruised. They took a moment to focus. Then she frowned. 'Zach?'

He nodded, suddenly not trusting his voice.

She dragged herself to her sock-clad feet and slowly walked to him as though she might be imagining him. He dug his fingernails into his palms to stop himself from taking the final steps and dragging her into his arms and kissing her for all he was worth.

'How's your father?' he asked.

She shook her head. Then nodded. 'He's had two

more attacks this week. He's lucid, his blood pressure is stable, but he's fading and refusing to go to hospital no matter what any of us say.'

Her eyes flickered at that last part, and he wondered if she'd been one of the ones suggesting it, or if she'd stubbornly kept out of his way.

She waved a hand over her face as though swatting away a fly. 'What on earth are you doing here?'

'You left in such a hurry. You were so upset. I couldn't let you stay away without knowing…' *God, this was much harder than telling Ruby how much he cared.* 'Without knowing I've been thinking of you.'

Day and night. Night and day. He'd been sure he'd heard her laughter around the resort, caught her jasmine scent.

The sound of real laughter, children's laughter, spilled through the window and like a mother hen Meg upped and headed out through the French doors to check see. Zach followed.

From the small balcony he saw Ruby sitting on Mary's lap watching Meg's nieces, clad in fairy dresses and tiaras, running around the backyard flying kites. Below, sitting in matching white cane chairs and drinking iced tea, like something out of *The Great Gatsby*, a slew of other Kellys— brothers, sisters, uncles, cousins, grandparents— watched on.

'You brought Ruby *here*?' Meg asked, her voice thin, her hands gripping the concrete balustrade as if she were preparing to vault down onto the lawn and whisk Ruby away from the clutches of her family.

He understood why she'd resisted the idea of having children. But she was made to be a mum. She was a natural protector, an instinctive defender of those who couldn't defend themselves. As a child she might not have been able to fight back when she was pushed down, but now? Now she was a warrior.

As far as he saw it, the only thing standing in the way of her fighting for her own happiness with as much purpose as she did so for others was fear. A broken-down ego was a fragile thing. Not easily repaired. He just had to make her see how strong she had become.

He said, 'She overheard me explaining to Felicia that your dad was sick. She wouldn't let me visit without her, or we would have been here sooner. She wanted to make sure you were okay.'

'Me? Is she okay?' Meg asked, her eyes glued to Ruby. 'I mean, is this making her think too much about her mum being sick? I'd hate to be the one to bring all that back up again.'

'She's fine. She's curious. She's amazing, really. Tough when she needs to be, and soft when she can be.'

Just like you, he wanted to say, but he knew she wasn't ready to hear it. Yet.

Meg spun on him, a ghost of her usual spirit flashing in her eyes bringing colour back to her cheeks. She shoved a finger into his chest, backing him into the shadow of the doorway. 'Do you have *any* idea how many reporters are camped out on the other side of your gate?'

'I drove in that way,' he said calmly, 'so, yes.'

'They're not as dim as they look, Zach. They'll have seen you. They'll have seen Ruby. They'll know who you are. They'll figure out who she is. She's cute, and funny, and female and your sole heir. They'll eat her alive. Didn't you hear a word I said?'

He reached out and held her upper arms; she calmed instantly, blinking up at him as if she were really seeing him for the first time. Her energy coursed through him like a wildfire and he wanted to kiss her so badly he had to grind his teeth to distract himself.

'I'm fully aware of all that,' he said. 'But I'm done hiding. I'm not going to teach her that's the best way to live because it's not. We've decided that life can come at us from any angle now and we'll take it on together.'

Meg blinked at him. She felt so small, but so warm, beneath his hands. She was his match, his inspiration, someone he wanted to know everything about, someone he wanted right beside him as he leapt into the new chapters of his life.

As a five-year-old his happiness had been in the hands of strangers; as a thirty-five-year-old his happiness was his to reach out and grab.

'So in that same vein, here we are,' he said, emphasising each of the last three words.

At the last second he held back from adding, *And we're yours if you'll have us.* She'd work it out. She had to. All it had ever taken for them to understand one another was a look.

He lifted a hand to run the backs of his fingers gently down her beautiful cheek. And saw the moment she understood when a flare of awareness lit her dazzling blue eyes. The same flare ignited in his stomach.

He swept a curl from her eyes. Then another until his hands cupped the sides of her face. He could practically taste her, feel the soft fullness of that mouth against his.

Suddenly she twisted out of his grasp, turned her back on him, and walked back into the room.

'Has anyone offered you a drink? Would you like some lemonade? James has made bucketloads and it's magic. Really. He could sell the stuff and retire rich and never have to open another door for any of us again.'

He took a step towards her, arm outstretched. She slid gracefully behind an ottoman.

'Meg.'

She breathed deep and sank down onto the

ottoman, as though she was so tired of fighting she could no longer stand.

He moved towards her. She held out a hand using the international sign for *back off*, and it stopped him in his tracks.

Her voice came to him, husky and defeated, as she said, 'Last weekend my family had been trying to get through to me for half an hour but I'd turned off my phone. I was heading to be with you and Ruby and it was easier to pretend they didn't exist if I wanted to believe that I could have what you have—a clean, fresh, new start.' She looked up at him. 'But this is who I am. This is where I need to be.'

'That's nonsensical.'

'Excuse me? Now I'm *nonsensical*?' She turned on him with such rancour in her eyes he backed up a step.

'*You're* not nonsensical,' he shot back, not giving her a chance to break eye contact. 'You're a human dynamo. You're an inspiration. You care so much for other people I know you don't take near enough time to care for yourself. And you've been a small miracle in my life. But believing you deserve to suffer right along with your father is ridiculous. You're punishing yourself for his mistakes.'

She blinked at him, her lips thin, her eyes raging. But at least she was listening.

'You've given me enough words of wisdom—it's

my turn. Family *isn't* a given. It wasn't for me, and in the end it's not for you. Family is a choice. Because deciding who to share your life with is a choice, and those you choose to spend your life with are your family. Love the Kellys you love. But just because they are a vital and somewhat Herculean force in your life needn't ever stop you from stepping away and creating your own family.'

'Zach, it's not that simple.'

He took a careful step her way. 'All that ever stopped me was me. Ruby came along. I chose to take her into my life. And look at me now. All that's stopping you is you.'

She swallowed hard, her chin tilting as he came closer. 'I'm not you.'

'And for that I'm eternally grateful. But I'm also not your father. Ruby's not you. Ruby's not your niece. And you're not your father either.'

He sank to a crouch close enough he could touch her if he just reached out his hand. But even though it killed to do so, he held back. 'Meg, sweetheart, I came here today because it has become all too clear to me this week that you are my family. I choose you.'

Her eyes softened. Hope sprang within them. Until she shook her head. 'Well, you can't have me. You don't want me anywhere near your daughter.'

Zach's jaw clenched. *Now* she was being nonsensical. 'Meg, I told you, I'm past that. You helped me get past that. And Ruby adores you—'

She shook her head harder. 'Zach, please. If she's anything like I was at sixteen you'll lose half a head of hair.'

'Let me worry about my hair.'

She spun on the ottoman so her knees faced him square on. 'Then worry about this. I ditched school at sixteen. I went clubbing every night. I drank daiquiris like they were lemonade. They let me in because of who I was, because of who my father was. When I chipped this tooth on a champagne flute I was sitting up front at a comedy bar, already on my second three-hundred-dollar bottle. *Sixteen years old.* That same night I was pulled over for drunk-driving, driving without a licence, under age, and a bag of pot was found in my glove compartment. I had friends in the car with me. Friends I could have killed had I not been stopped. Friends who for some reason are still my friends today. That could have been the end of me, but somebody put pressure where it was needed and I was let off with a warning. Somebody paid off every paper in town so that none of it ever came to light.'

'Somebody,' he said, still trying to filter the rest. 'Somebody meaning your father.'

She breathed in deep, ragged breaths. Her hands began to shake. He placed a gentle hand over hers, but he wasn't sure she even knew he was there.

Her voice sounded so small as she said, 'My trust fund wasn't meant to be mine until I was twenty-five. It was signed over at eighteen. I figured it was his way of finally washing his hands of me. That same day I approached my first doctor. But even I, with my glorious name, and glorious money, and batting baby blues had to wait until I had undergone six months of intensive therapy before a doctor would agree to—'

Her words ended on a choke and that was when his confidence took its first tumble. 'Agree to what?' he asked, needing to know even though he knew he'd regret it when he did.

'I've had my tubes tied, Zach.' She looked up at him then, at the end of her rope. 'It's irreversible. I can never have kids.'

Holy hell.

If Quinn Kelly weren't on death's door Zach feared in that moment what he might have done to the man.

Meg stared at him as if she half expected him to shake her senseless. Or run as fast as his shoes would carry him. But all he wanted to do was to take her in his arms and hug her. To hold her until she absolved herself. Until he got his head around what it meant to him. Until he stopped thinking what might have happened had Isabel done such a thing and Ruby had never been born.

'Aren't you going to say something?' she said, her voice tight, angry, desolate.

Zach ran a hard, fast hand over his face. What the hell could he possibly say?

'Zach?'

He stood and paced in a tight circle. 'I need a minute.'

'I should never have told you.' She shook her head so hard he was sure her brain must have been knocking against her skull.

'Hang on now, Meg. You know you've just thrown me a hand grenade there and I get the feeling you're certain I'm about to run for cover. I'm not, but I still need a minute.'

She stood and paced on the other side of the ottoman. 'You didn't have to know any of it. Nobody ever did! But you had to appear in my life and be all unimpressed by it and make me like you. And then you had to add Ruby to the mix. And then more and more and more of you. There. Everywhere. Not letting me have a minute to think about what we were doing. So if this—' she waved a hand over her chest '—is too hard for you to take, it's your own fault!'

'Meg, you picked the wrong man to try to push away. I'm not running. Not any more.'

'But see now, that's the thing. You are still running. You just don't know it,' she said, her voice suddenly so calm he wondered if he'd ever been in control of the conversation, even for a single second.

Zach brought his back foot to rest beside his front, feeling as if he needed to be upright for what was coming. 'This ought to be good.'

'That morning, at your house, Ruby gave me the card she'd made me.'

'The card?' *Oh, hell, the card.*

'The pink card with the chocolate muffin picture and the fur and feathers and glitter.' She swallowed before saying, 'The one you wouldn't give me yourself.'

Zach stood rooted to the floor as the import of that one small choice sank in. At the time it had been a split-second decision. An insurance policy, protecting his daughter and himself, that one last, tiny little bit.

In the end it might have cost him everything.

When he said nothing, Meg continued, 'Last week was something crazy. Something amazing and wonderful and I'll never forget a second of it. But the card only proved what I already knew—that you're nowhere near ready to take on the likes of me.'

Zach shook his head. The both of them were so adept at talking themselves into whatever they wanted to believe, this was all about to go belly up on the back of circular conversation.

He shut down reason and went purely on instinct, knowing if there was ever a moment to trust in the man he'd become this had to be it.

'Watch me,' he said, then shoved the ottoman out of the way with a foot and gathered her into his arms. As though she'd been holding herself up by nothing more than will power she collapsed against him.

He kissed the top of her head. The edge of her ear. The lift at the edge of her lips.

With a sigh she tilted her head and kissed him back, her lips clinging so gently, so tenderly, so lovingly to his.

It took all of his strength not to lift her in his arms and carry her to the couch and prove to her in the most basic way that he was right and she was wrong.

Far too soon she pulled away, looking down so he couldn't see into her eyes. He snuck a finger beneath her chin and made her face him.

Her chest rose and fell. Her eyes were as wild and blue as his lake amidst a summer storm. 'Why don't you hate me for what I did to myself?'

'Because I know why you did it.'

'Remind me, please. Right now I'm struggling to come up with a good excuse.'

'You made sure nobody could ever reject you again as fully as you rejected yourself.'

She swallowed and a big fat tear rolled down her cheek. He brushed her hair from her eyes and breathed through it lest he join her.

'God, you were eighteen,' he said, his voice rasping through his tight throat. 'You were still a kid. Those blasted doctors should be hung. But it would be impossible for me to ever hate *you*. How could I when I love you so very much?'

Her eyes glistened, flickering between his. He'd said it. He'd told her. He was her safe place to come home to.

He thought he had her. Until she held out her hands in supplication. He could see in the utter transparency of her expression how much it meant to her.

It just didn't matter.

He let her go as though his fingers had been burnt, rather than his heart. She wrapped her arms back about her body and headed back over to the French doors to watch the interplay below from a safe distance—the only family she thought she deserved, the kids she'd convinced herself she'd never have.

'Please stay as long as you want while Ruby's having such a good time,' she said, polite as could be. 'James will show you out.'

There was nothing more he could do or say. He did as she asked and walked away.

He'd spent his adult life protecting himself from just this situation, from blindly loving someone with no guarantee they'd love him back. But Meg had smashed through that wall with all the subtlety of a wrecking ball, convincing him he'd found someone worth the risk.

As he jogged numbly down the steps with gen-

erations of stubborn-chinned Kellys watching on he
realised the one thing he hadn't considered was that
for her the risk of loving him might yet be too great.

CHAPTER THIRTEEN

As THE sun set Meg sat out on one of the white cane chairs looking over the now-empty back lawn, the divine sound of kids just being kids echoing in the back of her mind.

The rest of her felt like toast. Three-day-old burnt toast that had fallen butter-side down on the kitchen floor and been kicked into the dust-filled gap beneath the fridge.

Zach had come to her daunting family home and left his precious daughter playing outside with her nieces as though if they were her blood they could do no wrong. He'd looked more dashing and beautiful and terrified than she'd ever seen him look. He'd offered himself up to the press, he'd heard her last and most devastating of secrets, a secret that meant she could never give him the kind of family he was ready for, and he'd still told her he loved her.

There was nothing more he could have done to

prove himself as the man she'd known he could be. And still she'd sent him away.

'Sweetheart,' her mother said, a hand curving over her shoulder. 'Are you coming in for dinner?'

Meg smiled up at her mother and stretched until her tight muscles began to feel useable again. 'I'll be in in a minute.'

She felt her mum's hesitation. 'Your father's alone right now if you wanted to have a chat. I'd noticed you haven't been in to see him since you came home, and I thought, perhaps, now might be a good time.'

Meg stilled, then tucked her feet onto the chair and wrapped her arms about her knees. Her mum was right about one thing: there was no time like the present. 'Mum, can you sit for a minute?'

Mary sat, perched on the edge of the seat as though ready to take flight. It made it easier for Meg to say what she needed to say, as she was almost sure her mum knew what was coming.

'Mum, I don't much want to talk to him. And I think you know why.'

Mary clasped her hands together until the knuckles turned white. 'Darling, he's so sick, surely you can—'

'Mum,' she said gently, but it was enough for her mother to close her lips.

Meg leaned forward and took her mum's hands in hers. 'You know how he treated me when I was a kid.' Even using the endearing term 'Dad' felt wrong. It always had.

Mary said, 'He's exacting, and puts as much pressure on all of you as he always has on himself. His work was so much more stressful back then. The business was in its infancy. His father was hard on him too. And everything he did was for the betterment of the family.'

Meg nodded along. She'd heard it all before. 'Is that why the two of you had me? For the betterment of the family?' She swallowed. 'To keep the family from falling apart when Dad had an affair?'

Mary opened her mouth to deny everything, then something in her changed, relaxed, as though she didn't have the energy to keep up the pretence any longer. She took a hand and cupped it under Meg's chin. 'You always were the most sensitive child. You were a blessing at a time we needed one most. But you can't only blame your father. We both did things we shouldn't have done.'

'*You* had an affair?' Meg asked, sitting up so straight so fast her back cracked.

Mary nodded, her eyes filling with tears. 'It was short-lived. It was foolish. But in the end only good came of it as it proved to both of us that we were where we wanted to be after all. We chose to be a family again.' She reached out and tucked a curl behind Meg's ear. 'Having you after that was the best choice I've made in my life.'

A choice. Meg had always wondered if she'd been a stopgap measure, never looking at it from the angle that she'd been a purposeful *choice*. The massive delineation rang so loud in Meg's ears she almost couldn't think. But it was fighting hard against the clang of another. 'Am I his daughter?'

Mary's eyes grew wide with shock. 'Of course you are. Look at you. You have his eyes. You have his pluck. You certainly have his temper. Your sweet temperament and endless capacity to forgive are definitely from my side.'

Her mother leaned forward and kissed her cheek. 'Now that's the last we need to hear of that. Don't be long. Dinner's on soon. And your father is still up there alone.'

Meg nodded, but stayed put as her mother walked away.

Forgiveness.

Zach had forgiven his foster parents for their weaknesses for the sake of his own family. Her mother had forgiven her father for his trespasses for the sake of her family. Her father had never forgiven himself and self-condemnation left only bitterness in its stead.

Meg had to forgive herself the unhealthy choices she'd made at sixteen. The desperate one she'd made at eighteen. Only then could she fully embrace the many exceptional choices she'd made since then. The keeping of friends she'd had since school. Being an integral part of her family's success. For unreservedly giving to those far less fortunate than herself.

For falling in love with Zach.

That had to be just about the smartest thing she'd ever done in her whole life. He knew her. He understood her. He loved her. But even more importantly, he'd helped her to realise how far she'd come in knowing, understanding and loving herself.

Could he ever forgive her for abandoning him? Could she ever forgive herself? Before she had room to find out, there was one last person who needed to see how far she'd come too.

Late that night, after a typically long, noisy, combative Kelly family dinner populated by her mum, all her brothers and their significant others, a dog-tired Meg made her way back up the stairs, past the wall of beautifully framed, lovingly tended family pictures, and she slid into her father's room.

Flat against the wall she could hear his uneven breathing. Flat against the wall she wasn't going to be able to do anything. She walked to his bed, and sat carefully on the edge.

He looked old. Frail. His skin was like rice paper. Even his eyelids were wrinkled. Like this he seemed so harmless.

He flinched, then looked into her face with his fierce blue eyes and turned a not too happy shade of pink as he bellowed, 'Jeez, child, could you have snuck in here any more quietly?'

'Don't shout!' she shot back, moving hurriedly to sit farther down the edge of the huge bed. 'You'll pop something and I doubt I'm the one you'd want trying to plug it up.'

He tried to sit up, failed, swore to the high heavens, and then slumped gingerly back onto the huge mound of pillows. 'What on earth are you doing here, girl? I was informed you were whooping it up on holiday.'

'I've been back a few days now.'

'Not for my sake, I hope.'

'No. Of course not,' she said, her voice droll. 'The girls were one down on their backyard cricket side. I had to come back for the sisters.'

His eyes were entirely clear when he said, 'You've never been any good at cricket.'

'Mmm, so you've taken great delight in telling me on numerous occasions.'

Quinn scoffed. 'Would you prefer I butter you up? Resting on your laurels never helped anyone.'

'No,' she said. 'You've made well sure my laurels have never given me any rest.'

And there it was. Back to square one. The two of them watching each other cagily from opposite corners of the ring.

Meg flattened a sock-clad foot on the ground, preparing to get out of Dodge, when it hit her that heading out that door meant nothing would have changed.

Unless she could make the break from her past she'd end up playing the 'It-Girl' for ever. Brushing off her blonde wig every time she did the kind of work that really gave her satisfaction. Dating men who never challenged her. Trying to pretend that Zach Jones never existed. Trying to convince herself that sharing every piece of herself, her fears, her joys, her body, her soul with him had been nothing but a holiday romance.

Not good enough. Not any more.

'Dad.' She reached out and took his cool hand. It stiffened, but she didn't let go. 'It appears my Kelly blood runs deeper than I even knew. I do believe I'm going to miss you.'

'Gallivanting off again, are you?'

She almost laughed. Stubborn old fool. Instead she took his words at face value.

'I will, in fact. I'll be taking leave of my Kelly duties for a bit.'

She would? *Yeah*, she thought with an inner sigh of relief, *she would*.

He glared at her as though she'd said she was renouncing her name, her religion, and the old country just to be contrary. She raised both eyebrows and glared right on back.

'The thing is, Dad,' she said, 'I currently volunteer at the Valley Women's Shelter every week. Have been doing so for some time now. It's tough, it's terrifying and I love it madly. So much so I've decided my PR work for the family is going to have to slot in around that from now on rather than the other way around. In fact, I might even take a social work course, which would cut into that time even more.'

He opened his mouth, no doubt to cut her down twenty ways from Sunday. She held up a hand and said, 'Not this time. The decision's been made. And there's more. I'm in love, Dad, with an amazing man who knows everything about me—everything—and he loves me anyway. Can you believe it?'

She could hardly believe it herself, but saying the words out loud finally made it all utterly, beautifully, intensely real.

'I'm tired, child,' he said, turning away. 'Can't you have this conversation with your mother?'

'I will in good time. But I wanted to have it with you too. For *you* to know that I've reached a point in my life when I feel as though I might just be really, really happy.'

'And you need to tell me this now in case I don't wake up in the morning?'

She lifted an eyebrow. 'That's exactly why. So now you know. Your daughter has turned out just fine.'

He looked her in the eye, for the longest time she could ever remember him doing so. His eyes, so very like hers. His inability to forgive so far removed from hers. Then he settled deeper into his pillows and looked up at the fringing hanging off the canopy bed as though it held more interest than anything she'd had to say.

'Fine,' he said. 'Now I know.'

It wasn't congratulations. It wasn't an act of contrition. Yet Meg felt her oldest wounds beginning to mend.

A soft rap on the door was followed by James's face poking through the gap. James slipped into the room with a box of Krispy Kreme doughnuts.

She opened her mouth to rouse at James, then let it fall shut. She wasn't her father's keeper any more than he was hers. So without another word she just hopped off the bed and walked out, pretending she hadn't seen.

Feeling as if she were living a good inch higher off the ground than she had been her whole life, Meg floated into her old bedroom, grabbed her handbag, fixed her hair, swiped on some lip gloss, spritzed on some perfume and continued floating down the stairs.

She passed the library where the family had gathered for after-dinner drinks. Dylan called out, 'Get in here, kiddo. I want to run through next week's schedule. There's a dozen odd things I need you to do for me.'

Her shoes touched solid ground. Telling Dylan he'd have to find someone else next week would take all night.

She caught James the butler's eye as he eased silently into the room from another door. And seeing her escape, mouthed 'sorry' then said, 'Did you know James is feeding Dad doughnuts?'

Brendan made to scold, but Cameron got in first, laughing his head off. And as their collective attention was diverted Meg took her chance and escaped.

And then she was gone, jogging down the dark front steps of the manor two at a time, the rush of summer air blowing her hair off her face, making her skin tingle, making her lungs feel open and free.

Or maybe it was the thought of a man with dark chocolate eyes, adorable curls, warm, strong arms, enough chutzpah to put her in her place, and a capacity to love her despite knowing the worst she had to offer that had every sense feeling as if it was truly alive.

She hopped into her Jag and burned down the Kelly Manor driveway, spinning gravel in her wake.

Only when Meg hit the locked gates outside the Juniper Falls Rainforest Retreat did she realise she hadn't exactly mapped out any kind of plan.

She simply pressed the intercom. A sleepy voice answered. 'Juniper Falls Rainforest Retreat, how can I be of assistance?'

'Hi. Meg Kelly here. Can you, uh, by any chance, wake Zach Jones and tell him I'm here?'

After a pause the voice said, 'I sincerely wish I could, Ms Kelly, but you are not down on my sheet as being expected.'

'I know. And I'm sorry about that. But this is a surprise visit. Of sorts. A last-minute but long-overdue kind of thing. You see I'm here to…'

To what? Oh, to hell with it. Zach had laid himself bare for her, to her family, to the press, to his little girl. If she was ever going to prove to him she was right there with him, she had to do the same.

'I've come to tell him that I'm in love with him!'

The gates whirred open instantly. She crawled through to find two men grinning at her from their booth. One doffed his cap, the other blushed like mad.

'Take the route around the back of Waratah House past the garage,' one said, 'and keep on following the fence line. You'll practically drive straight into Mr Jones's private carport. Good luck!'

She gave them a jaunty salute and spun off, feeling high as a kite, and as terrified as if she were in the middle of one of those walking-down-the-middle-of-the-Queen-Street-Mall-naked dreams.

But there was no backing down now. Her secret love was out there for her father and all Zach's staff to know. There was nothing, *nothing*, stopping her but herself, and herself was pressing down hard on the accelerator.

* * *

Zach was waiting by the garage at the side of his house wearing nothing but thin, faded, cotton pyjama bottoms when Meg's noisy old car zoomed up, lights on high beam.

He hated to think what had brought her here, tonight, at such a time. He reached for her car door and opened it before she'd even come to a stop. 'Meg, don't tell me your dad—?'

She half stumbled out of the car. 'He's fine. He's the same. But we talked. Well, I talked, he pretended not to listen. And it felt like letting out a sour, stale breath I'd been holding for almost thirty years. The next breath in was…ecstasy. I could never have done that without your encouragement. So first I have to thank you for that.'

He opened his mouth to try to slow her down, but she kept on going.

'I talked with my mum too. Boy, did so many things become clear. Even you'll be shocked. Or maybe not. I've probably used up your shock quota for the year by now. Or maybe I'd just been locked up inside all week and what I needed was fresh air and sunshine to see things clearly. You taught me that too. So thanks again.'

She looked up into the sky, arms outstretched, breathing deep, then seemed to realise the velvet black sky was littered with stars. She frowned.

Worried Meg might be about to spontaneously combust, Zach took her by the elbow and walked her to the octagonal pool house around the side of his property. Once inside the snug room he turned on a lamp, and placed her on a bamboo love seat.

Her entire, beautifully nubile body jiggled. He clenched his hands at his sides and struggled to keep his eyes on her face. 'I hate to ask,' he said, 'but have you been drinking?'

She looked up at him, all big blue eyes and pink cheeks and red lips raw from being nibbled at. Or had she put on make-up since he'd last seen her? Lip gloss, rouge, mascara, perfume? Had she done that for him? His fingers unclenched a very little.

'Coffee,' she said. 'Loads and loads of coffee from a couple of drive-through places on the way. I haven't slept much in the past few days and I needed to be awake for this. And since I wasn't actually sure that you had coffee on hand, or if you'd merely been using the promise of coffee as a lure all this time—'

She shook her head, seeming to realise she hadn't taken a breath. Then she gingerly reached out and took his hand and gently drew him down onto the seat next to her.

His fingers gripped hers and pleasure flooded through him. It seemed that even after she had put him through one of the most gruelling and sobering afternoons of his entire life, his body was not nearly as immune to her as his brain would have liked.

'Meg,' he said, his voice gravelly, 'it's after midnight.'

'It is?' she asked, looking around as if she only just realised where she was.

'I'm usually used to functioning at this hour, but it's been a very long day.'

'Tell me about it.' Her eyes swung back to his. Warm, inviting blue. Calm, settled blue. Vivid with a great purpose blue. A tiny ray of hope split the night. At least it felt like hope. Hope wasn't something he'd experienced all that much of in his life, but it felt good whatever it was.

Not sure he could stand to have it dashed twice in one day, he asked, 'Did you have a particular purpose in coming all the way out here?'

She turned his hand over and placed her palm against his. It was cool and small and light. He ached to pull it to his lips and kiss it for the longest time. But the purpose in her eyes was something he did not want to divert.

'I don't quite know where to start,' she said. 'I feel like I'm on daylight savings time. It all made such perfect sense about an hour and a half ago.'

He took a calming breath. 'What did?'

'That you came to the house today to tell me that you loved me,' she said. 'And for some great daft muddle of a reason I tried to convince you that it wasn't the most glorious news I'd ever heard.'

Zach's heart lurched. Gloriously.

'You love me,' she said again, shuffling closer. 'You, Zach Jones, love me. You love me enough to give me the space I needed to confront my past so that finally I could see further than a designer-shoe-clad foot in front of my own face, which was as far as I'd dare look into the future for such a long time.'

He did. And he had. On the drive home he'd realised she needed more time. And that he'd wait for her as long as she needed. A half a day was as good as he could have hoped.

He did what he'd been aching to do since the moment she arrived and slid a hand around the back of her neck. 'I must be crazy, but I do truly love you.'

'You do?' Her voice was so soft and unsure, her eyes so big and bright, Zach did all he could do and laughed.

His heart felt like a rocket ready to take off. The countdown had begun inside him the moment she'd hopped out of the car and if she didn't reciprocate and soon he was going to explode. 'If you have any feelings for me whatsoever then you'll put me out of my misery and fast.'

Her blinking slowed and, as was her way, she looked him dead in the eye. At the same time she laid a gentle hand on his cheek and it was all he could do not to ravage her on the spot.

'I've lived with a debilitating fear of rejection my entire life. I combated it by being whatever I had to be to be loved by as many people as possible. You made me feel like I actually had to earn your respect. And when I did my opinion counted as much as yours, if not more because it was fresh and new. For those reasons and about a trillion others I do love you.'

She needn't have said another word for the rest of time. But being that she was who she was, she kept on giving.

'I love that you own a million health resorts, but have a thing for chocolate muffins. I love that you push my buttons leaving me nowhere to hide. I love your eyes, your arms, your bare feet, and the crease that appears in your right cheek only when you laugh. But most of all I love that you are ambitious, and hard-working and wilful, but it took less than half a second for you to change your entire life for the sake of one small girl. You are a unique specimen amongst men. And I love you so much my heart is full to bursting with it.'

The rocket inside him went off, filling the last of the empty places inside him with nothing but warmth. 'You have no idea what it feels like to hear you say that.'

'So tell me.'

He laid a matching hand on her cheek, her softness seeping into him, melting away the last of his sharp edges. 'After so many years spent not be-lieving love was in store for me, I'm still halfway stunned that I actually believe you.'

She nodded. Glanced at his lips. Licked her own. Then swung her legs so they rested atop his. His soft cotton pants did nothing to hide the stirrings beneath.

'So what now?' she asked, her voice a husky whisper in the darkness.

'Are you kidding me? Do you want a play by play?'

She pulled back and gave him a look he feared he was going to be on the receiving end of for a very long time. 'I meant we aren't the only ones affected by this.'

'How about we keep the press release in the drawer for a few days yet?'

'Don't be smart. I meant Ruby and you know it.'

'She made me pancakes, but she never made me a card. I have the feeling you're going to be a big hit. And as for your other concerns, you have to remember she comes from tough stock.'

She raised an eyebrow. 'You think the Kellys aren't tough? They suck you in and there's no getting out. Dylan and Cameron are intractable and they've both managed to convince perfectly lovely women to be with them. And you took one look at me and you were gone. Kellys are competitive, ambitious, opinionated, defiant—'

'Sweetheart, they're you.'

'Me? I'm a marshmallow.'

'Nah. You just do it prettier.'

'Zach—'

'She'll be fine. Honestly. And at the first sign she isn't then we'll deal with that then. Okay?'

She thought about it a moment, then nodded.

'Though,' he said, 'there is one other way to fix any concern you might have over your family's influence over our girl.'

'How's that?'

He twirled her hair between his fingers. 'Don't be a Kelly any more.'

She shook her head so hard her hair fell in messy waves over her shoulders. 'They may all be as mad as March hares, but I do love them too.'

'Of course you do. Anyone who stepped foot inside that behemoth of a house of yours would see that as a clan you're just about unbreakable. But that's not what I meant. I mean you wouldn't be a Kelly any more if you changed your last name to Jones.'

'Very funny,' she said, slapping him on his bare chest. He clutched her hand to him and her fingers curled against his bare skin. 'So is now a good time to admit you're not the first person I told?'

He waited for his offer to sink in, but she was obviously still too wired. 'That you love your family?'

'That I love you!'

'Dare I ask?'

'I kind of let it slip to the two security guards who let me in.'

Zach laughed. He laughed so hard the windows of the tiny thatched pool house shook. 'Then again,' he finally managed, 'what's the use of one more secret? Everyone's going to find out eventually.'

'They will?' she asked.

'Marry me and there's no stopping them.'

Her eyes grew as big as saucers and he knew this time she'd heard him.

'You can't just say something like that to a girl, especially one in my highly caffeinated state.'

'I can and I will.'

'You really want to marry me? Even knowing everything you know? Even though I can't...' She swallowed down an obvious lump in her throat. 'I can't give you any more kids.'

Zach knew better. He'd Googled like a madman the minute Ruby was asleep. The operation she'd had was irreversible. She couldn't conceive naturally. But it didn't rule out IVF. He knew she'd have no idea because she'd have been too terrified to check. But now wasn't the time for that. They'd get there when and if the time was right, as they seemed to get to everything else when they were good and ready. Only this time he'd make sure they'd get there together.

'Meg,' he said, running his thumb down the side of her face, 'I certainly don't want to marry anyone else.'

'Ah,' she said, her voice getting wobblier by the second. 'The last of the great romantics.'

'How's this for romantic?' He took her hand, lifted it to his lips and left a gentle trail of kisses up each finger and across her palm. Her eyes fluttered closed and her mouth fell open. He took advantage, pulling her to him and kissing her for all he was worth.

She melted against him, warm and languid, and he had not a clue how much time passed before they fell apart.

She gripped his upper arms for support and her famous blue eyes fluttered open, looking into his as if she'd just had some kind of religious experience. God, he was going to love being with this woman.

He asked, 'Tell me that's a yes.'

She snuck her arms around his torso and hugged him tight, her chin resting on his shoulder, her words sliding against his ear. 'Yes.'

Yes! He mentally punched a fist in the air.

He said, 'We are never going to be able to live this down, are we?'

'What's that?'

'Meg Kelly, heiress, society princess, only daughter of the Ascot Kellys, the Kelly Investment Group Kellys, marries orphan-made-good Zach Jones.'

'Did you have any idea I could be so magnanimous?' she asked.

He laughed. Warm all over now, and only getting hotter every second, she wiggled her body further atop his.

'But first,' she said, running a finger in circles over his bare chest, 'before we go one step further, we need to get some things straight.'

'Honey,' he said, sliding a finger along the

neckline of her stretch T-shirt. 'Believe it or not I'm worth double what you are. A pre-nup wouldn't be worth the paper it's signed on.'

Meg breathed out long and slow and finished with a smile that hovered halfway between beatific and a threat. 'Kellys don't do pre-nups. Kellys do for ever.'

Zach's next breath matched hers. *For ever*. Never ever did he think he'd see the day when he believed in for ever. But as he let his hand slide over her shoulder and more firmly down her back until she curled like a cat, he couldn't wait for for ever to start. 'So what do we have to get straight?'

Her eyes fluttered closed. 'I've jogged my last. I refuse to let wheat grass touch my lips ever again. And there is no way I'm getting up before the birds every day. Not even for you.'

'And chocolate, and coffee…'

Her voice was breathy as she said, 'Will for ever be a staple in my diet. You want me, you take my predilections.'

'Oh, I want you all right,' he said, stealing a kiss on her beautiful pale neck.

She shivered. 'And are you sure you really understand that you get my family too. They live over an hour away, but they aren't backwards about dropping in unannounced.'

'I actually liked your family, those I met anyway. Your mum was wonderful with Ruby.

Truly. And your brothers are all sporty types, right?'

Her eyes opened in time for her to roll them. 'They'll see you as manna from heaven. Thank goodness for Rye and Tabby and my new sisters-in-law, all sensible indoor-type women.'

'Thank goodness for indoor-type women everywhere.' He reached out and switched off the lamp.

'Well, what just happened there?' she said into the darkness.

'Just in case,' he said. 'Guests have been known to come wandering to this part of the resort on occasion.'

'How impolite.'

'How indeed.'

Thankfully the moon was not obscured by a single cloud so he could still make out Meg's shape, her soft curves, her smile. He kissed the end of her nose. The corner of her lush mouth. The curve of her cheek. When he found the edge of her ear lobe her head lolled back on her neck as though her muscles had turned to liquid. 'You're too easy.'

'Try playing me at any board game on the planet and you'll be singing another tune, my friend.'

Instead he chose another indoor game, which left them both winners.

And afterwards, scads of coffee or no coffee, Meg fell asleep on the floor of the pool house, wrapped in his old, warm, soft, favourite, red, woollen blanket and in his arms. Her face peaceful, the dark rings beneath her eyes gone.

Content. Happy. Home.

EPILOGUE

Six weeks after making Juniper Falls her home, and a little over a month after Quinn Kelly's colossal and extremely moving state funeral—attended by no less than three foreign heads of state—Meg stood waiting at the gates of the Juniper Falls resort. Her high ponytail bounced about her shoulders as she hopped on the spot, and her hot-pink high heels kept getting stuck in the grass.

She glanced down at her brand-new engagement ring—a pink diamond solitaire as chosen by fashionista-in-the-making Ruby—glittering beautifully on her left hand and thought for about the hundredth time that her life couldn't feel any different than it had two months before.

Quite apart from becoming more at home with her spectacularly beautiful new digs, her new man, and the new little girl in her life, she was still attending sporadic events as Meg Kelly, the face of the Kelly family, ones she had hand-picked herself. She was still volunteering at least twice a week at the Valley Women's Shelter, only now she did so without any kind of disguise, internal or external, and the satisfaction it gave her had increased a hundredfold.

But this day, at the beginning of the next to last week of the summer school holidays, she was going to work for her new family's business.

A big white bus finally came through the Juniper Falls gates. It had barely pulled to a stop when what seemed like a thousand kids spilled out. Bedraggled urchins the lot of them. With dark eyes all but popping out of their pale faces as they took in elegant Waratah House and the lushly encroaching rainforest.

Meg clapped her hands loud enough for the group to quiet down. 'Okay, guys, I need you to do me a big favour and get yourself organised in one long line, alphabetical by first name.'

'What if two of us have the same name?' a big kid with a missing front tooth asked.

'Excellent question. Then the one with the longest big toe goes up top. Right?'

A couple of kids whipped off their shoes and holey socks, just in case.

Meg grinned. 'If you have it done in five minutes, there's ice cream waiting for you in the restaurant.'

The loudest whoop she'd ever heard had her holding her hands over her ears and running for the side of the bus as the kids frantically introduced themselves to one another, which was the actual point of the exercise.

After the bus driver, whom Meg waved up the hill towards food, Zach was the last to hop off the bus. He looked as raggedy and wide-eyed as the rest of them. After an hour's trip up the mountain with this lot she wasn't surprised.

She sidled up to him and wrapped her arm around his waist. 'There's my big, brave, manly man. You survived.'

He said, 'The week's not over yet.'

Together they watched the Juniper Falls ground crew, headed by Felicia—now the resort's official Children's Activities Co-ordinator as well as Ruby's some time babysitter—keeping the kids whipped into an eager frenzy.

'I never thought I'd say this, but thank goodness Ruby's a reader not a runner,' Zach said.

Meg bit her lip. She knew better. The first time she'd seen Ruby she'd been swinging up a storm, her clothes covered in evidence of further adventure. But that was another mystery her dad would never have to know about. Now there was an extra pair of eyes looking out for Ruby, eyes experienced in the ways of feisty young girls, those mysteries ought to become fewer and further between.

Meg laid a hand on Zach's chest. 'I've babysat Brendan's girls a thousand times. Believe me, let them run it out and they'll sleep where they fall come dark.'

'From your mouth to God's ears.'

They watched on in silence as the rowdy kids walked single file towards the restaurant.

'Can you believe they're really here?' she asked.

Zach shook his head.

An idea Zach had thrown out over dinner one night had become Meg's obsession. The whole week at the resort had been booked out for a hundred pre-teens, some treading water in the foster system, others from families who'd been through Meg's shelter.

Zach had put out word within the Olympic fraternity and several well-known athletes would run them ragged. The resort's staff would teach them things like how to resolve issues with words not fists. Rock-star mates of Meg's were to host a couple of dance parties, celebrity chefs to cook up healthy, fun food. And they'd be spoilt rotten.

But best of all, exposing these kids to Zach's story, and subsequent success, would broaden the horizons they dared to reach for. Exposing Meg to these kids had already broadened hers more than she'd thought possible.

She leaned her head on his shoulder as a mass squeal of delight echoed from the restaurant.

Zach said, 'I hate that Ruby's missing this.'

'She'll be back in a couple of days, so she won't

miss much. I know I've said so a hundred times, but thanks for letting Mum have her. Ruby will be a brilliant influence on Brendan's girls, and having all three girls has been the highlight of Mum's month. She's promised not to mention croquet lessons, or Baroque appreciation classes or a course in *commedia dell'arte*.'

Zach nodded silently, his back ramrod straight.

'You've got used to having her home these holidays, haven't you?' she asked.

He slid a hand over her hair, tugging the end of her ponytail, and nodded.

'Yeah,' she said. 'Me too. We don't really have to send her back to school next week, do we?'

He kissed the top of her head. 'You're the one who came from the good family—how did you end up being the bad influence?'

'I'm Libran. I will do anything to make people love me.'

'Mmm, and there I was thinking people couldn't help loving you just because you're you. And all along it was the accident of your birth.'

'Happy accident?' she asked, looking up at him again.

He appeared to think about it for a moment. Then two.

Meg moved to pinch his arm, but he caught her hand in time and held it behind her back. Heat slid through her centre, the kind that still caught her off guard after all these weeks, the kind she didn't see herself ever getting used to.

And then he kissed her with the kind of sweet, sensitive, all-consuming passion she never planned on getting used to.

Eons later they pulled apart when the sound of big tyres crunching against the white gravel drive split the peaceful silence.

The next of the four remaining buses was pulling in, and Dylan's harrowed face was peering out the front window. Tabitha bouncing about next to him the likely reason.

Meg grabbed Zach's hand and pulled him inside the first bus. They jogged to the back bench seat and hunkered down with Meg atop Zach's lap, her arms about his neck so that they could watch from a covert vantage point as Tabitha, Dylan and his fiancée, Wynnie, attempted to corral their group.

'You should have let Rylie do a series on her TV show about what we're doing here this week, you know,' Meg said. 'The publicity would have been amazing.'

'It would have. If we wanted publicity.'

The public figure and the private benefactor in Meg both struggled to be given free rein. 'But think of the fundraising opportunity—'

'I have more than enough funds to do this any time I want.'

She sat up straight. 'As do I. But I wish the world knew what an amazing man you are.'

'So long as you know, and Ruby has a vague sense of it, and your family suspects, then the world can think whatever it wants.'

'You know what else?' Meg asked, curling closer. This way I get to keep you all to myself. And talking of having you to myself, how many sleeps till we head off to St Barts for the Grand Opening?'

'Ah, twelve.' He ran a finger down her nose before sliding it beneath her chin. 'We still have time for it to be a honeymoon instead, you know.'

Though the idea felt just as thrilling now as the first time he'd suggested it, she knew that she wanted her family, her whole extended family, to be a part of the happy day when it finally came.

'A quickie wedding?' she said. 'A four-day honeymoon? Sometimes I think you don't know me at all.'

The finger beneath her chin moved to slide behind her ear and she struggled not to purr.

'Fine. Then when we get back,' he said, his voice gentle, 'can we continue that talk from the other night?'

She nodded. Her next breath in shook. And then she smiled. 'We can do better than that. I made an appointment with a fertility specialist at Monash VF in Melbourne for not long after we come home. They practically invented the procedure, so if we're going to start finding out the possibilities of maybe one day having another child, then that's where we start.'

Zach leaned in to plant a kiss on her lips. Talk about heart-warming. 'No matter what happens, always know I'll always love you.'

She kissed him back. 'Always know I'll always love you too.'

He nodded. Promise sealed. He moved in for another kiss, when Meg stayed him with a finger.

'I just had a horrible thought,' Meg said, biting back a grin.

Zach's eyes narrowed. 'Do I really want to know?'

'What if Ruby asks for *commedia dell'arte* classes?'

'I'm not going to be the one to say no.'

'Yeah, me neither. They were actually kind of fun. Oh, look.'

The next bus pulled up and Cameron and his wife, Rosie, stood at the front clapping madly and singing some travel song they'd forced on the poor kids in their bus.

'You know what else is fun?' Zach said, nuzzling against Meg's ear.

She turned back to face him. 'Do I really want to know?'

Zach slowly pressed Meg down against the leather seat, waved at her the keys he'd used to lock the bus door, and grinned. 'Yeah, you really want to know.'

FREE ONLINE READ!

The Cinderella Valentine
by Liz Fielding

Don't miss this short story linked to the
BRIDES OF BELLA LUCIA
novels.

 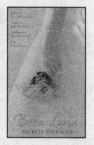

To read your free online story, just go to:

www.millsandboon.co.uk/cinderellavalentine

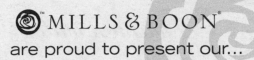

A wanton widow

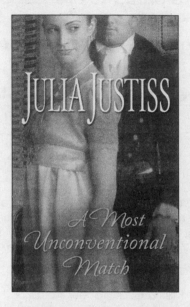

Hal Waterman has secretly adored newly widowed Elizabeth Lowery for years. When he calls upon Elizabeth to offer his help, his silent, protective presence awakens feelings in her that she does not understand.

Elizabeth knows that society would condemn her, but Hal's attractions may well prove too much to resist!

Available 16th April 2010

A collection of three powerful, intense romances featuring sexy, wealthy Greek heroes

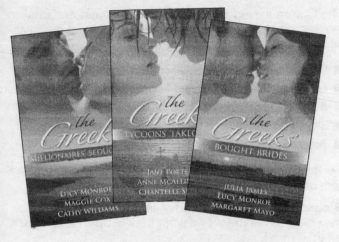

The Greek Millionaires' Seduction
Available 16th April 2010

The Greek Tycoons' Takeover
Available 21st May 2010

The Greeks' Bought Brides
Available 18th June 2010

millsandboon.co.uk Community

Join Us!

The Community is the perfect place to meet and chat to kindred spirits who love books and reading as much as you do, but it's also the place to:

- **Get the inside scoop from authors about their latest books**
- **Learn how to write a romance book with advice from our editors**
- **Help us to continue publishing the best in women's fiction**
- **Share your thoughts on the books we publish**
- **Befriend other users**

Forums: Interact with each other as well as authors, editors and a whole host of other users worldwide.

Blogs: Every registered community member has their own blog to tell the world what they're up to and what's on their mind.

Book Challenge: We're aiming to read 5,000 books and have joined forces with The Reading Agency in our inaugural Book Challenge.

Profile Page: Showcase yourself and keep a record of your recent community activity.

Social Networking: We've added buttons at the end of every post to share via digg, Facebook, Google, Yahoo, technorati and de.licio.us.

www.millsandboon.co.uk

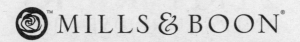

2 FREE BOOKS
AND A SURPRISE GIFT

We would like to take this opportunity to thank you for reading this Mills & Boon® book by offering you the chance to take TWO more specially selected books from the Romance series absolutely FREE! We're also making this offer to introduce you to the benefits of the Mills & Boon® Book Club™—

- **FREE home delivery**
- **FREE gifts and competitions**
- **FREE monthly Newsletter**
- **Exclusive Mills & Boon Book Club offers**
- **Books available before they're in the shops**

Accepting these FREE books and gift places you under no obligation to buy, you may cancel at any time, even after receiving your free shipment. Simply complete your details below and return the entire page to the address below. You don't even need a stamp!

YES Please send me 2 free Romance books and a surprise gift. I understand that unless you hear from me, I will receive 5 superb new stories every month including two 2-in-1 books priced at £4.99 each and a single book priced at £3.19, postage and packing free. I am under no obligation to purchase any books and may cancel my subscription at any time. The free books and gift will be mine to keep in any case.

Ms/Mrs/Miss/Mr _____ Initials _____

Surname _____

Address _____

_____ Postcode _____

E-mail _____

Send this whole page to: Mills & Boon Book Club, Free Book Offer, FREEPOST NAT 10298, Richmond, TW9 1BR